The Perfect Elizabeth

The Perfect Elizabeth

A Tale of Two Sisters

Libby Schmais

THOMAS DUNNE BOOKS
St. Martin's Griffin
New York

THOMAS DUNNE BOOKS
An imprint of St. Martin's Press

www.stmartins.com

Design by Heidi Eriksen

Library of Congress Cataloging-in-Publication Data

Schmais, Libby.
  The perfect Elizabeth / Libby Schmais
      p. cm.
    ISBN 0-312-25225-0 (hc)
    ISBN 0-312-27080-1 (pbk)
    1. Young women—Fiction. 2. Sisters—Fiction. I. Title.

PS3569.C51515 P47 2000
813'.6—dc21   00-024759

10 9 8 7 6

To my sister

Acknowledgments

FIRST OF ALL, I want to thank my fabulous agent, Neeti Madan, of Sterling Lord Literistic, and my wonderful editor, Melissa Jacobs, for their efforts on my behalf. I am grateful to Sam for all his love and patience, my family for their support, and Debbie for her endless readings and pep talks. I would also like to thank Martha Hughes and all the members of the Peripatetic Writing Group for their insightful comments and ongoing encouragement.

The Perfect Elizabeth

Chapter

one

A PHONE IS RINGING in the distance. I don't want to wake up yet. I am having a wonderful dream about a large apartment where everything is white, the whitest of whites. Music filters into my consciousness and I open my eyes. The digital clock glows greenly at me. I am listening to light music. The letters glow 7:48 which means it is really 7:18. My clock is a half hour fast in the hopes that seeing the later time when I am not fully awake will propel me into action. It hasn't yet.

For a moment, I achieve consciousness and sum up the situation. It is my birthday. I am thirty-two. I am listening to light music, my boyfriend is commitment phobic and I'm going to be late for work again.

Pounding on the snooze button I flip over, disappearing into sleep.

Seven minutes later, the phone rings again, insistently. I try to ignore it but it doesn't stop.

I stumble over my dresser and grab at it, rubbing what will soon be a bruise on my thigh.

"Hello?"

"Happy birthday to you, happy birthday to you . . ."

It's my older sister Bette. I am thirty-two years old.

"Stop, stop," I cry. "Listen, have I reached the age where I have to start whiting-out my age on my passport, like Zsa Zsa Gabor?"

"The sooner the better."

"I think I'll make this birthday the last one."

"Just remember . . ."

"I know, I know, all of life's problems can be solved by a hot milky drink."

MY SISTER IS writing her dissertation on nurturing in the English novel. Lately, she has taken to eating only the food in Barbara Pym novels, and she is forever inviting me over for a nice cup of tea or a boiled egg on toast.

"Don't you think all this food is a little bland?" I asked her the other night, over a meatloaf-like thing she insists on calling mince.

"That's the whole point, it's nonthreatening."

MY SISTER AND I cling to each other, like survivors of an unbelievable, strange event, an event that we don't have the words to describe. That event was our childhood.

Our childhood wasn't strange in the way other people's were. We weren't abused or tortured or locked in a basement. We had parents who were successful and intelligent, but completely out of our reach. If we had a problem, they were the last people we would turn to. We see each other frequently, although sometimes the last person you need to see is someone who has gone through what you have. We are different from other people, lacking in certain qualities, overflowing in others.

2

MY SISTER AND I weren't always close. There was a time when the five-year age difference between us was an enormous barrier. I used to look at her and see a distant emissary from the land of cool. In high school, she had a brown suede jacket with fringe that I wanted more than anything. Later, we started to confide in each other. When I broke up with Charles, she was the only one I could talk to about it. Now, when I look at her, I see myself, but different. I know that if she is OK, then I could be.

MY SISTER IS happy in her job. I've never had a job I liked. When I started my current job as a legal secretary, there were all these procedures to remember—client codes, computer codes, legal terminology. Now that I know what I'm doing, I think my job is easy, my knowledge useless. This is what I believe: Everything I know how to do well is useless. Everything that I don't know is impossible.

MY SISTER SITS in an ivory tower eating baked beans on toast. She has even persuaded her distinguished university to add it to the menu. I imagine her growing thin on a diet of Jane Austen and George Eliot. She believes (although she won't admit it) that she has had her one great love and all that kind of thing must be avoided from now on. She trusts novels not life. In novels, things work out according to plan; in life the plot is entirely unmanageable. I want to shake my sister into action. I want her to fall in love.

HANGING UP THE phone, I try to trace the origin of our dilemma. My sister and I grew up believing that our parents knew everything and everything they didn't know was irrelevant. They dismissed the ordinary as ridiculous, the spiritual as

3

unnecessary. They were communists in their youth. They hid people, secret people. When we tried to pin them down, the stories evaporated. They would become impatient, changed the subject. When I heard about them hiding people, I imagined an underground railroad like the one we learned about in middle school, with trapdoors and trick panels and slaves singing freedom songs.

In Westchester, having achieved tenure and membership in the heavily chlorinated community swimming pool, my parents drank two vodka and tonics every night and were your basic liberals. My mother is a professor at Columbia; my father teaches group psychology at NYU. Of all the people I know, they are the most open-minded. The only thing they truly abhor is the ordinary.

*M*Y PARENTS MET at a playground. They were young, athletic, Jewish and communist. They believed only in the rational. In a rather conventional series of events, they courted and got married. I know all this because I've seen their wedding album, which I found on top of a pile of psychology books in the attic. It's a sugary white photo album where they are young and beautiful, idealistic, and in love. There is a heart-shaped portrait of them gazing into each other's eyes, another picture in the shape of a candle where they are cutting the cake. I am always mesmerized by the last picture. The picture is in the shape of a keyhole. My father has my mother in his arms and they are waving goodbye, as if they are disappearing behind a door. I would go over this picture in secret, tracing around the keyhole with my finger, and look at my mother's white dress, in its tissue paper mausoleum. I tried to peer inside the keyhole, learn the secret that would make me understand these strange, powerful people, but they were always waving good-bye, shutting me out behind that closing door.

DURING MY CHILDHOOD, I was convinced I was going mad. I heard noises in my head, mostly a high-pitched buzzing sound. When I was twenty, a doctor told me this was not uncommon, something to do with the bones developing in the inner ear, but at the time I was too worried about my sanity to tell anyone. My parents collected objects with strange faces, masks, gargoyles, African sculptures. Before I went to sleep, the gargoyle heads on the banister outside my room would make faces at me in the half-light. I couldn't close my door because I was afraid of the dark but if I left it open, the gargoyle heads would see me.

I CAN'T REMEMBER my childhood as a whole but I do remember specific incidents. I remember a snowy day in March when I was in second grade. My brother and sister were sitting around the kitchen table listening to the radio announce schools that were closed. I remember praying for mine, and my brother grinning evilly at me, with the knowledge that his school started a half hour later than mine did and I had to leave first.

I asked my father, "Do I really have to go?" knowing the answer, as I pulled on my green rubber boots and zipped up my parka with the fuzzy white hood. We were only allowed to stay home in three specific instances: if we threw up, had a fever, or the radio said our school was closed.

Pulling on my mittens, I walked outside to the familiar path I took every day. Except that day, there was no path, only an endless blurry snowscape.

AT FIRST, I felt exhilarated. Everything looked magical and new and I played in the snow, touching it to my tongue, watching my feet make deep impressions in the untouched surface. But the further I got down the hill, the more strange everything seemed to get. The woods were unnaturally quiet, quiet and unfamiliar. It was still snowing and I was starting to get cold. When I got down to the bottom of the hill, I didn't know which way to go. The snow was so deep I couldn't distinguish any familiar landmarks. My house was out of sight and snow was seeping into my boots. The trees, which moments ago had looked magnificent and glittering, were now taking on a more threatening appearance; their snow-colored limbs seemed to be trying to grab at me, and in the tree trunks, I saw the hideous grinning faces of gargoyles.

I kept walking faster, feeling like I was going in circles. My mittens were wet, my hood was wet, and my feet were nearly soaked. At one point I tripped and fell, and I felt like lying there and crying, but I knew I had to get up or I'd end up frozen in the snow for eternity.

FINALLY, I EMERGED out of the woods into a clearing and saw something familiar, a building—Kingsley Elementary School, my school. I was so happy I ran as fast as I could to the main door, longing for school as I never had before, but when I opened the heavy door, it was quiet except for the sound of my boots dripping on the floor. I was the only one stupid enough to come to school in the snow. I heard a shuffling noise from deep within the school and I ran outside, not waiting to see who or what it was. It had stopped snowing, so I could make out my footprints and I followed them back, as fast as I could, all the way up the hill to home.

WHEN I FINALLY got back to the house, I opened the door and heard laughter. It was as if they hadn't even known I was gone. They were drinking hot chocolate in the kitchen, all of them, my parents and my brother and sister, as if nothing had happened. My father was at the stove, taking a survey as to who wanted matzo brei and who wanted fried salami and eggs.

"WELL, LIZA, I guess you know the good news. It's a snow day for all of us," said my mother, standing at the stove.

"Yeah, Kingsley came on the radio just after you left." My brother looked smug.

"You better get out of those wet clothes," said my father.

I REFUSED THE hot chocolate and all offers of food, as if denying myself would show them, and stomped up to my room, crying violently into my white parka. I barricaded the door with books and pillows but after a little while, I realized no one was going to come get me.

Just then, a knock on the door startled me. It was my sister. She had come up to see me.

She pushed at the door, but it was still barricaded.

"Liza, let me in."

"Okay, but just you."

She had brought me some hot chocolate. Unbarricading the door, I let her in.

M Y THERAPIST SAYS my entire name when I enter the room, Eliza Ferber. I think it's to make me feel like I exist. "Eliza Ferber," she says, and I lie down on the couch, mesmerized. When she says my name I start to like my name, a name that I have always found strange. My sister's name is Bette. Both of our names are diminutives of Elizabeth. It is as if we are the broken parts of one perfect Elizabeth.

*M*Y SISTER HAD one relationship, one very long relationship, a marriage, that ended, so now she believes that this avenue of endeavors, relationships, is permanently closed to her. How can you do something you have failed at? How can you try again? These are the concepts she and I have trouble with. I tell my sister she needs to meet someone.

"A nerd," I tell her over dinner that night at my favorite Italian restaurant, "or at least someone who was a nerd in high school and then blossomed later. They make the best boyfriends. They're so grateful to have a girlfriend at all."

Gregor, who is sitting next to me, shakes his head. "No, I don't think she should go for a nerd, she needs to play the field a little."

Gregor is my boyfriend. Actually his real name is Gregory, but he thinks Gregor is better for an actor, more unusual. We have been seeing each other for two years. He has blond curly hair and isn't my type at all. I used to go for all these tall, dark, foreign guys who never understood me. Gregor's more like me, grew up in the suburbs, reads books, thinks about things. Things are fine between us, but whenever I mention living together, he closes up like an oyster.

MY SISTER DOESN'T like the idea of the nerd kind of guy either. I can tell by her expression, as she picks at her spaghetti bolognese, a food that all English people eat when they go abroad. If she ever did like anyone, I imagine it would be someone with an air of mystery, someone dangerous, someone with secrets.

I compose a plan in my head of how I would meet someone if it came to that. I would take classes, exude an air of availability. But why would I have to? I glare over at Gregor as if he has already done something that has forced me into this course of action. Or would it be better to give up on this idea of togetherness, this happily ever after, once and for all? Why try to convince Bette of something I'm not sure I believe in? Maybe she is happier alone. She certainly looks happy, chatting with Gregor about desserts. She is describing a British dessert to him, jam roly-polies.

Before I get to order dessert, the waiters bring out a miniature chocolate cake for me, lit with two tiny pink candles. I feel like crying.

D O YOU THINK you would have your primary residence here or abroad?" I ask my sister a few days later. I am at her apartment and we are playing one of our favorite games: if I won Lotto.

She pauses from sniffing my small vial of peppermint oil, the latest in my series of attempts to lose ten pounds.

"Definitely abroad, do you think this works?"

"Yes, smell is intimately connected with hunger."

My sister and I are watching a British show about a monk named Cadfael who cures people with herbs and solves mysteries. I take a small piece of pizza to see if the peppermint oil is working.

"I would definitely live in Italy, Siena, in a small villa with dogs," I say with authority, biting into my pizza. It tastes so good I almost forget my job problem and my weight problem and my Gregor problem.

"With Gregor?" asks my sister.

"That is yet to be determined."

After we finish eating, my sister makes tea. She makes it carefully, using real tea, not tea bags, warming the pot, covering the whole thing with a tea cozy. Pouring out the Earl Grey into delicate china teacups, I continue with my Lotto scenario: "I would start the Eliza fund, scholarships for hopeless underachievers."

I WALK THE SHORT block home to my apartment, picking up a rejection letter from a small poetry magazine called *Output* and various credit card bills. The only good mail I get is a belated birthday card from my friend Elinor, who, after a string of horrible relationships, has left New York to start over in Boston.

Inside, I sink down on my maroon velvet couch I got at the Salvation Army. I look at the letter from *Output* more carefully. It's a form letter. *Thank you for submitting to Output, but your poem doesn't meet our current editorial needs. We are moving away from a traditional narrative structure.* Editorial needs? Narrative structure? Who needs them anyway!

I think of calling Gregor, but he is at acting class. Lately, he is always at acting class when I want to talk to him. I am convinced he will be a huge success, although he has only recently quit his corporate job to pursue this new career. I, on the other hand, will end up a large failure, although I have been writing poetry for years, even had a few things published in obscure yet prestigious literary journals.

I picture us at the Academy Awards, Gregor in a dazzling tuxedo, me in a figure-flattering black dress. We are spilling out of a limousine, or at least Gregor is spilling, or rather emerging from the limousine onto the arms of beautiful spokesmodels. I try to emerge gracefully from the limo but catch my high heel on a loose thread and tumble out to an ominous ripping sound. Luckily, the photographers have gone on ahead. Gregor looks back at me, concerned, but he is whisked away by thin women with cleavage.

I HAVE BEEN SNIFFING peppermint oil for two days now and my pants are still tight. I get ready for work, putting on a large white shirt over the pants, hoping it's suitably professional looking. I feel uncomfortable, bulgy, undisciplined. I fasten the top of the peppermint oil tightly and throw it in my bag.

I ARRIVE AND glide up twenty-seven floors to the spacious overdecorated law firm where I work. I remember reading somewhere that people choose offices with all the elements of their own dysfunctional family.

Darla, my boss, yells from her office, which is ten feet away from my desk.

"Can you believe this shit?" she says, pointing at a fax she received. I am tempted not to respond, but say, "That's terrible," having no idea what she's talking about but knowing that the one essential part of my job is responding.

She buzzes Tad, the only guy in the firm. When he doesn't answer on the first buzz, she becomes annoyed.

"*Tad, Tad*," she yells across the length of the office. "Where the hell are you?"

"I'm right here Darla," says Tad, rolling his eyes at me as he ambles into her office. He is wearing khaki pants and a cream-colored sweater. He is balding with a potbelly, but he affects a *Brideshead Revisited* look.

"I've been buzzing you all over," I hear her say, in the voice of a petulant girlfriend.

Three hours later, I sniff my peppermint oil and go out to lunch. I wander down the street, different food ideas circling around me like the dialogue bubbles in cartoons, pizza (bad), salad (good), Chinese (bad), turkey sandwich (good). I am supposed to be writing every lunch hour. I had vowed to devote the entire hour to writing poetry or the Great American Novel, but I usually waste my whole lunch hour trying to think of what to eat, and then feeling guilty for eating it.

I WALK BY the local farmer's market and buy a roll and some delicious sheep's milk Camembert that I've had before. I am addicted to cheese. In middle school, I used to carry little plastic bags of Parmesan cheese with me everywhere I went. Everyone teased me, but it made me feel safe. Cheese was always a joy, never disappointing. I would eat Kraft Parmesan cheese, pouring it into my hand from the green container, then licking it off. I would do this secretly, furtively, knowing it was something to hide.

I buy apples and consider pretzels. At Martin's pretzels, I stand in line and consider salted (bad) or unsalted (good).

"Liza, is that you?"

My first impulse, and this is always my first impulse when I hear my name, is to run the other way, but I turn toward the voice out of curiosity.

It is Alan, a friend of a friend, someone I slept with once around the time I started going out with Gregor, probably because Gregor was still sleeping with his old girlfriend, and I was trying to get back at him.

Alan looks the same, tall and intellectual with long, wavy hair. He plays drums in an atonal orchestra. He is looking at me carefully, and I wonder if he is thinking about the night the two of us were together. We drift slowly away from the pretzel stand.

"I haven't seen you in a long time," he says.

"Yes, it must be a couple of years." An image comes to my mind of Alan naked and I want to laugh. I can see him naked and me naked separately but it seems incredible to me that

12

these two naked images were ever superimposed on each other. We were with my friend Janet that night. Janet was fighting with her boyfriend and we all drank too much champagne and took a taxi back to her house to have a slumber party. After a while, Janet decided to go back to her boyfriend's apartment and I was left alone with her roommate Alan. I guess we ran out of conversation because I don't really remember being attracted to him. I didn't even want to stay there but it was three in the morning and I was too drunk to leave. He made up the couch for me and offered me a white T-shirt to sleep in. When he gave me the T-shirt, he kissed me on the neck. It's hard to remember exactly what went through my mind but I was feeling insecure about Gregor, and I wanted to be reckless. I remember Alan told me afterward I was "fun in bed." It made me feel like some kind of kid's game: having fun in bed with Eliza.

I offer Alan a pretzel in the hope that it's too difficult to think about sex when you are crunching on a sourdough pretzel.

We walk around the farmer's market. I point out my favorite stands as if I am a tour guide: "They have wonderful strawberry rhubarb jam over here, and over here, there's great apple cider."

"We should get together," he says when I pause for breath. "My practice studio's near here. We could have lunch."

"All right." I wonder if I should mention Gregor now or wait. Maybe it is presumptuous to assume that someone has designs on you because you and he once slept together.

"Well, I really should be getting back," I say nervously.

"It was nice seeing you." Alan looks at me in a way that makes me wish I had never had sex with him. I begin to under-stand how men can say "It meant nothing" and mean it.

"You look great," he adds, putting a heavy hand on my arm.

I say, "You, too," meaning it was nice seeing him too, not that he looks great, and hoping he knows what I mean.

13

I wave as I walk away. That wasn't so bad. He said I looked great. Well, it's possible. I look at myself in the window of a men's store and feel curvy and desirable. You look great Liza. I glide back up to my office on the elevator, clutching my Camembert and apple, imagining myself at a picnic in France, surrounded by admirers. *A little more Vouvray, darling? Yes, I don't mind if I do.*

M Y SISTER AND I meet for our weekly Sunday brunch at the Mansion, the diner equidistant from each of our apartment buildings. I can't decide what to eat.

"This is not a big decision," says my sister, exchanging a sympathetic glance with the hovering waiter.

"Which do you think is worse, a grilled cheese or a BLT?"

"Grilled cheese, they dip it in all that oil."

"I should have a turkey burger, that's healthy. But it might be really weird. How would you know what they put in it? Or a turkey sandwich. Do you see those?"

"Just order."

"Okay, okay, I'll have a grilled cheese and french fries. Oh, I bought a book for you."

Bette takes the book, reading the title out loud. "*How to Meet a Mensch in New York.* Liza, you're kidding!"

I flip through the pages pointing out highlights to her, singles parties, candlelight dinners, book clubs, even computer dating. There are tiny pen-and-ink drawings of couples lounging on the pages sipping cocktails.

"What's the matter?" I ask. "Don't you think it's a good idea?"

The food arrives with a clatter. Bette plays with her cinnamon toast. "No, I don't know. Maybe I'm not ready."

"Just read it, okay? You don't have to do anything."

"Okay, I will, thanks. So, how are things with you and Gregor?"

"Do you know that you change the subject just like Mom does?"

"I thought we were finished."

"For now. Anyway, we had another talk and Gregor said he'd be miserable if we ever got, you know."

"Married," whispers my sister dramatically.

I nod.

"To you, or married in general?"

"In general, I guess, but still!"

"What's wrong with him?"

"I don't know. I don't even want to get married, I just want to live together. He's the one who brought up marriage. He said he wouldn't want to live with anyone unless they were married. But he doesn't want to get married."

"A classic catch-twenty-two."

I eat the rest of my french fries one by one, dipping them into a pool of ketchup and then dousing them with salt. We order chocolate ice cream sodas for medicinal purposes.

"You can always come with me," Bette says, pointing to the drawing of a couple laughing at a wine-tasting party.

IT'S NOT AS if I always wanted to get married. In fact, I'm not sure I do now. But when you're with someone who so clearly doesn't want a particular thing, you start feeling rejected by them not wanting the thing you're not sure you want yourself.

Whenever we talk about the future, I get what Gregor calls "pre-sad." I imagine us already broken up, me at home, alone, watching old movies and crying, Gregor out on dates.

Gregor says he wants to be with me, that he doesn't want to be with anyone else, but he can't promise anything.

I wonder how you know if someone is right for you. The other night, Gregor and I were having sex, and all of a sudden I started laughing uncontrollably. Gregor was inside me and I couldn't stop laughing. He started laughing too, which made it better. And then we both stopped laughing and started having sex again and it was fine. More than fine. And that's the kind of thing that makes me think we should stay together.

FOR DINNER, I make pasta. Tuna fish, cream of mushroom soup and shells. I mix half the undiluted cream of mushroom soup with the noodles and stir in the tuna fish, topping it all with Parmesan cheese. This is my comfort food, the food of my childhood. Gregor thinks it is disgusting. I only make a small, diet-appropriate amount of noodles but after I eat it I am still unsatisfied. I make more, eating it quickly until I feel uncomfortable. I throw out the remainder of the noodles and the container of cheese. I can't be trusted with these foods.

WHILE I EAT, I read a Barbara Pym book my sister lent me. It's about these four middle-aged people, two men and two women. They all work in the same office, and it describes their lives as they drift into retirement and old age. I start thinking that I am not so different from these characters. How the years are slipping by for me too. I imagine my sister and I in some large dingy apartment, arguing about the right way to arrange the food in the cabinets, the events of our childhood, kind of like the Golden Girls from TV but less jovial.

I call my sister. "I think you should sign up for dance

classes. The fox-trot, the rumba and the merengue—or how about a singles party?"

"Maybe."

GREGOR CALLS ME at eleven that night. He's finished rehearsing with his scene partner and he wants me to come over. I tell him I'll think about it and call him back. I open my curtains and look out the window. It's so dark it's purple out, purple and raining, and the thought of going anywhere fills me with dread. I start the process of going over to his house in my head. Pick out all my clothes for tomorrow. Pack them up. Take a cab. Pay for the cab. Leave. Enter. Rain. Umbrella. Cold. Shoes. I open my closet door and look at my shoes and realize I can't go anywhere.

I CALL GREGOR back and tell him I'm tired. Hanging up the phone I feel sad but soon I settle in, take a long hot bath, and decide to finish the book about the four old people. Luckily there's a kind of happy part near the end, where the strangest of the four old people, the lady who collects milk bottles and tins of food, dies and leaves her house to one of the two men, and the three remaining former office workers meet for Tio Pepe at his house, opening up new possibilities of future social encounters.

I eat some raspberry sorbet, and its cool clean taste soothes my stomach and my nerves. Eating sorbet makes you feel thin. I curl up in my old chenille bathrobe with the rip under the arm. I'm glad I didn't go over to Gregor's. Maybe there is some hormone that makes me think I'll be happier living with someone. I'll take dance classes with my sister. We'll get frilly dresses and merengue with Latin dance instructors with pencil-thin mustaches.

17

Chapter two

MY SISTER CALLS me, panicked.

"There is a mouse sitting on my couch." The note of fear in her voice disturbs me. I want my sister to be more emotional, but I am critical of the emotions she has.

She was always the capable, practical one, and I am reluctant to let that expectation go.

Since my sister is so agitated, I pretend to be calm.

"Don't worry, I'll be right over."

I rush over to her apartment, feeling like a fireman, rushing to save lives.

WHEN I GET there, the mouse is no longer on the couch. It is scurrying along the white counter of my sister's sink. I see it out of the corner of my eye, a fuzzy shape, an irritation in my visual field.

"Bette, move very slowly. Do you see it?"

The mouse pauses, frozen. The mouse is not scary, just

pathetic, its small brown body shaking uncontrollably, not unlike my sister's.

"Yes, I see it," my sister moans, backing up from the kitchen. "Do something."

I advance toward the mouse holding a wineglass, with a vague idea of trapping it inside. The mouse, however, has other ideas and starts scurrying away.

I demand tools, a plastic bag and gloves.

"You're not going to kill it, are you?" asks Bette.

"Of course not. You know, if you keep having this problem, you should really get a humane trap. You put peanut butter on a cracker and the mouse waits in the trap until you let him out."

"Why not cheese? I thought they loved cheese, a nice Havarti, perhaps."

"No, you have to use peanut butter to lure them in, they respond to the smell or something."

"What's it doing, now?" The mouse is frozen again, so I walk toward it.

Moving very slowly, I lure the mouse into the plastic bag, pushing it gently with the tips of the black leather gloves.

"THE WHOLE BUILDING is infested," my sister says, her voice becoming higher and higher. "They must be exterminating somewhere." She hovers in the kitchen while I get the mouse into the plastic bag and the plastic bag into a larger shopping bag.

"Sssssshhh!" I say sternly. "Calm down."

WE TAKE THE mouse outside to the little park near her house and put the bag down behind a bush. I cut the plastic so the mouse can crawl out. We do this in a secluded spot where no one can see us, as if we are doing something illegal.

After we free the mouse, we decide to go the Mansion

Diner for some medicinal carbohydrates. We order rice pudding with whipped cream.

"Bette, I didn't know you were so scared of mice."

"Yes, you did. I've always had this phobia," says my sister. "It's just we always had cats and dogs who scared them off."

AS WE EAT our rice pudding, I say, "You need someone who can deal with these problems."

"Does Gregor deal with mice?"

"No, he's useless with any kind of insect or rodent. He's more scared than I am." I grab a copy of the *New York Press* and start leafing through the personal ads. "This is what you should do."

We read the ads and Bette jots down ideas. "I don't know, they're full of so many adjectives. What adjective do you think I'm like, hypothetically?"

"Let's see. You're hypothetically intelligent. Quirky. But you're my sister. It's hard for me to be objective."

"What would I put down for looks—average, attractive, pretty?"

"You're definitely pretty." I am embarrassed. We are not given to dispensing compliments freely in my family. I grab the pencil from her. "Okay we'll say 'v. attractive.' How's that. Do you want to say sexy?"

"No, they'll think I'm a slut."

"Okay, we've got 'very attractive, intelligent, SWF,' should we say academic?"

"No, too intimidating."

"Well, it's true. You know, I can't believe you never meet anyone at school."

"They're all self-absorbed academics. Anyway, I'm shy."

"What are you seeking?"

"Handsome, intelligent, I don't know."

"I've got the perfect line: "No Rollerbladers, no Republicans.' "

21

"That's good, but I'm not sure I can do this, Liza. It's humiliating."

"Do you want to meet someone?"

"Yes, but I want it to be special."

"It can be special later."

A WEEK LATER, MY sister and I enter a ballroom downtown, in the Flatiron District, uncomfortably close to where I work. We are going to a singles party. My idea.

My sister and I are dressed hopefully, in short skirts and glossy lipstick. I look around apprehensively. What if I see someone I know? I look up at the ceiling, as if I am here to admire the architecture.

We reach the blond wooden desk, with the blond guy behind it handing out flyers for Club Med. They're raffling off a trip later.

"I am *not* wearing a name tag!" my sister proclaims to me sotto voce.

"Welcome," booms the man behind the desk. He is obviously used to reluctant entrants into the singles world, people pretending they are not really here for this singles party, although it is the only event happening in the building at this time.

"Come on in." He points us into the main room. "We're creating a group of young people at the bar, around that pillar."

"I guess that means he thinks we're young people," says my sister, my older sister, although for this event I have told her she can say she's younger if she likes.

I give her instructions: "Just remember, you don't know anything about the sixties or seventies. You are a child of the eighties. Think punk, not disco." We can't help but think disco with the strains of "Disco Inferno" blasting out from the makeshift dance floor.

We enter the bar area, the "young area." Unfortunately, the men here have a striking resemblance to the guys you find lurking around a bus station, people you move away from, not Prince Charmings.

My sister and I exchange a horrified glance.

"I guess being in the young area is less of a compliment than we thought."

Don't make eye contact," I whisper. She complies and we walk quickly toward the bar and stand there immobile, unable to commit to even ordering drinks. The bartender, young and oily, grins at me.

"This your first time here?"

I nod.

"Here, I'll buy you a drink." He hands me and my sister two enormous daiquiris stabbed with little white umbrellas.

He winks at me. "It gets good between seven-thirty and eight."

I look at my sister's watch, but it is barely six.

"Thanks." A man who looks like a small, not-green version of the incredible hulk comes toward us and asks my sister to dance.

"I can't," she says politely, as if she has a medical condition that prohibits dancing.

"It's cool. I'll see you round." He thuds away.

We try not to laugh.

I sip my drink, which is too sweet and too strong. "Let's go."

We leave quickly, threading our way through the crowd, until we are out on the street, breathing deeply. We see several other women leaving at the same time, attractive women. They look at us and we all groan simultaneously.

"Wasn't that awful?"

"Never again."

"Oh my God."

MY SISTER AND I recover from our experience in a dark pub, drinking foreign beers.

"Sorry."

"It's hopeless," sighs Bette into a Belgian white beer.

"Look, this was a nightmare, but that doesn't mean it's hopeless. You were in a relationship for ten years. It takes time to recover. It takes half the time you were in a relationship to recover from it."

"Where do you get these numbers? If that's true, I've still got a few years left before I have to do this again."

"It doesn't mean you can't meet someone else in the meantime, while you're recovering. Listen, I read somewhere that in order to meet someone, you have to take a bath with an unbroken raw egg. The egg soaks up all your negative energy."

"An egg?"

"Trust me."

Chapter three

N MONDAY, I meet the new secretary in my office, a guy. He reminds me of Burl Ives, only younger. He wears a scarf with piano keys printed on it.

"So, what do you do for fun Liza?" he says, looming over my desk.

"Oh, the usual," I respond, looking at my computer screen intently.

At the coffee machine, he asks me, "Do you have family in the City?"

I try to be polite. "Well my parents live in Woodstock, although they teach in the City, but my sister lives near me, so we see a lot of each other."

"Is she married?"

I shake my head.

He smiles widely. "So you're both single?"

"Actually I'm involved with someone."

This doesn't seem to stop him, and after lunch he comes in and gives me a small bag of pretzels from the farmer's market.

"There are two things that get to me: pretzels and pretty girls."

I don't meet his eyes. "Yeah, pretzels are great."

I always feel uncomfortable when guys I'm not interested in flirt with me. I end up being too mean or too nice, not knowing how to hit the proper balance. With Stan, I find myself veering in the too-mean direction.

LAST NIGHT I dreamt that Robert De Niro asked me to be the spokesperson for Lancôme cosmetics. I agreed, on one condition. They had to photograph me head-on. "Not in profile," I kept saying, louder and louder, until I woke myself up.

If I asked my mother to interpret my dream, she would say something like, "You want to be in control of the way others see you," and I would feel she hadn't understood me at all.

My mother is a dream therapist. She teaches in a doctoral program at Columbia University. I haven't told her my dreams in a long time.

At work, the receptionist buzzes me with a phone call. It's my father. He tells me that last night, my mother had a vascular incident caused by the New York Times. But my father didn't call me until today, twelve hours later, when they knew she was going to be okay.

Last night, while I was dreaming of Robert De Niro, my mother was in the hospital, hooked up to machines in the emergency room.

My father called to tell me from a pay phone and over the street noise I heard, "Liza, your mother's had a kind of attack. Her blood pressure shot up, and we're in the emergency room at NYU. But she's okay. Don't worry."

As I write down the address of the hospital, I feel as if the floor is slipping beneath me.

My mother's attack happened at the American Dream Conference, the ADC. My mother was a keynote speaker and right before she went on, someone handed her an article about the elimination of her department due to budget cuts and she started to feel dizzy. She already knew about the budget cuts, but seeing it in print must have made it seem official.

"It wasn't really the *New York Times* article," says my father. "It could have happened at any time."

"Doesn't it seem like an incredible coincidence, that she reads about herself in the paper and then collapses?"

"I suppose." My father is reluctant, even now, to attribute emotional causes to physical events. He does not support the notion of the mind-body connection, at least not in his family.

"By the way, Liza, we have two theater tickets for tonight, for a Terrence McNally play. Since we won't be able to use them, I thought maybe you and Gregor might want them."

"Dad, I can't think about that now."

WHEN I GET off the phone my first impulse is to not tell anyone. To stay in control. Not to cry.

Tad walks by my desk and raises his eyebrows. "What's the matter, forget to take your medication?"

I hear him from a distance and smile vaguely instead of responding. I decide I have to be very careful, try not to make mistakes, be nice to everyone, until my mother is out of the hospital.

My sister calls me and we speak softly, timidly, as if we are already orphans, clinging to each other for survival tips.

"It'll be okay," we say tentatively.

"Call me as soon as you know anything."

27

My FATHER IS protecting us from information about my mother's condition, but it is information we crave, information that makes us feel safe. I long to rush out to Barnes & Noble and look up high blood pressure and dizziness in heavy medical dictionaries, to cross-reference. I want to go on-line, hear the reassuring click of the printer spitting out relevant articles and abstracts.

I can't picture my mother in the hospital. I can only see her light-headed and dizzy at the dream conference, surrounded by women in flowing outfits with multicolored scarves. These are the same women who have surrounded her since I can remember, my mother's colorful, overflowing dream friends. I imagine my mother falling in slow motion, clutching the *New York Times*, her life's work wiped out by those gray smeary pages.

I vow never to read the *Times* again.

I have to tell my boss, Darla, about my mother so I can leave early. I postpone it until the last possible moment. When I tell her, it all comes out in a rush: "My mother's in the hospital I need to leave early it's my early day anyway her blood pressure keeps shooting up my father still wants to go to the theater."

I start to cry. Darla takes me by the shoulders and pulls me toward her. I don't want to be hugged. I feel suffocated. Darla is large and hugging her is like being pressed against a sleeper sofa. Extricating myself, I rush out of the office.

I feel disoriented, the way I felt when I heard of my house burning down over a scratchy transatlantic phone line, while I was spending my junior year of college in France. I called my home number and there was a long pause, and then Elaine, my mother's best friend, answered the phone. Apparently, all their calls had been transferred to her house. When she realized who I was, she said, "Liza, I have some bad news for you."

28

Her voice sounded blurred and I kept thinking, This is a bad dream. I'll tell my mother about it later and she'll interpret it for me.

Later, once I accepted that our house was gone, burned to the ground, that this had really happened, I started thinking it amazing that disasters didn't happen all the time. I started expecting car crashes when I walked across the street, every rash to be the sign of an incurable disease.

I walk fast in the direction of the hospital, expecting the worst. It's raining and I try to get a cab. It is impossible. I walk and the feel of the wet dark rain against my skin is reassuring. As a kind of prayer, I don't put up my umbrella.

W HEN I ARRIVE in the emergency room, my father is sitting in the waiting room grading papers.

"Hi Liza, how are you? How was work?"

I feel exasperated by his calm. "How's Mom, is she going to be okay?"

"They want to do some tests, rule out various possibilities."

"Dad, did you tell Daniel?"

"Not yet."

Daniel is my brother. He lives in Guatemala and appears in our lives infrequently. My brother is a healer. My parents aren't sure what to think about what he does. It's too close to mystical for them. They laugh nervously. "Our son, the Jewish shaman," my parents say at dinner parties, wondering how it happened.

I'm not sure exactly what my brother does, although he's tried to explain it to me. I know he heals people, in unorthodox ways. He is currently working with bees. He calls me every couple of months to check in.

"If you walk into a swarm of bees," he told me on the phone recently, "you can get amazing results."

"That's a big if," I said.

My father is trying to protect Daniel from this knowledge about my mother. When something bad happens, we find out later. When the house burned down, my parents didn't call me right away. When I called and found out, it was already two weeks later.

"Dad, you really should call him."

"I will."

MY SISTER ARRIVES and we fidget on the vinyl seats of the waiting room while my father grades papers. On the dot of six o'clock, the huge double doors open and a large guard waves us in. We are only supposed to go in one at a time, but the guard nods for us to follow our father, putting his fingers over his lips so we'll keep a secret.

My mother is lying in a hallway hooked up to a heart monitor. It bleeps periodically. She is flushed, but sitting up in her hospital bed doing the *Times* crossword puzzle, in pen. She looks tired, more tired than I have ever seen her. I always forget how thin my mother is. She has long gray hair pulled back into a ponytail and pale blue eyes. Her students have always loved her, tried to make her their family, and sometimes I felt there wasn't much left over for me. The way she looks at me from her white metal bed with the heart monitor bleeping overhead, I know she loves me and I long for magical powers to make this all go away.

They are wheeling in beds all around her, old people who look half-dead already, strange people, like the woman next to my mother who keeps laughing, although nothing funny is going on.

I notice my mother still has blue eyeliner under her eyes from last night. It is slightly smudged. She must have put it on for her speech. My mother hardly ever wears makeup, maybe sometimes a dab of lipstick for a meeting. She wears ethnic clothes, textured, draped clothing. Clothing that is like a costume.

"You're wearing makeup."

"From last night," she says slowly. I dip my finger in a cup of water and carefully rub off the blue smudges.

"So Liza, you want to use the theater tickets?" interjects my father.

"No."

"Are you sure?"

"Yes, I'm sure."

My father seems disappointed that I'm not going along with his plan. It's as if he believes if we go to the theater, if we see Terrence McNally's play that got such a good review in the paper, things can't be seriously wrong.

My sister stands nervously by the bed, telling my mother she'll bring her Dorothy Sayers mysteries, shortbread, special homeopathic remedies. My sister is more optimistic than me. She is sure there will soon be a bed for my mother, that doctors will appear and give her a diagnosis. I believe the doctors know nothing, that the unthinkable will happen.

At the gift shop, my sister and I become giddy and pick out gummy bears and peppermint patties. My father paces suspiciously around the store, as if the gift shop is a foreign planet, as if he's never been in a gift shop before. He asks the sales clerk if they have *The Nation*, but she just stares blankly at him.

I want to get my mother *People* magazine but I check first with Bette.

"She wouldn't let herself read that," Bette says firmly.

I pick up a large stuffed dog. "Wouldn't it be funny if we came back with this?"

"Hey, Dad, what about *Vanity Fair?*"

"She wouldn't like that."

"Have you ever read it?"

31

He shakes his head and we get it anyway.

When we get back to my mother, she has finished the puzzle and holds it up proudly.

"Even here," she says, "I can finish the puzzle."

"Maybe you should lie back," I say. She looks red and blotchy. I imagine all her blood rushing up and down like an out-of-control elevator.

"Liza, I'm fine sitting up."

She gives my father instructions on whom to call. Tell so-and-so that I won't make my class; cancel my appointment with so-and-so . . .

How do you make someone who can't relax relax?

MY FATHER AND I take the subway home together for a few stops. He is staying at their new apartment in the City. He tells me he is playing tennis in the morning, his usual foursome.

"What are you going to tell them about Mom?"

"I don't think I am going to say anything about it."

"Dad, they're your friends."

"Liza, it's not the right setting, we're just there to play tennis."

It's so typical. My parents can't admit any weakness. Depression, failure and illness aren't allowed. Everything has to be fine.

WHEN I GET home, I am restless. I spend an hour washing the shower curtain. It's blue, an ocean scene of fish and plants and orange coral, but it is encrusted with dirt. I unhook it and wash it in the sink with

Murphy's Oil Soap and Top Job over and over again until it is clean.

I know I won't be able to sleep in my apartment so I decide to go over to Gregor's and wait until he comes home from acting class. Recently he's given me keys, but I have never just gone over uninvited. Gregor obsessively checks his answering machine, so I leave a message to let him know I'll be there.

AS I AM about to sink into sleep, I hear Gregor's key in the lock and his soft step as he tries not to wake me.

I wake up anyway and he makes me chamomile tea. He is glittering with acting electrons, his hair flying around excitedly.

While he holds my hand, I tell him about my mother. He traces my fingers one by one. He tells me it'll be OK and I try to believe him.

I sleep fitfully, dreaming of ice formations and scientists.

THE NEXT DAY, my sister and I don't hear from our father all day. We don't go out for lunch. We wait by our respective phones, in our respective offices. I imagine my father has had a sympathetic heart attack and can't get to the phone, which is just out of the reach of his unconscious hand. We call each other at two-hour intervals.

"Nothing."

"Nothing."

AFTER WORK, WE meet at the emergency room, and in the waiting room, we see my father with a bag of take-out Chinese food.

33

"Oh hi," he says.

"Why didn't you call us?"

My father looks puzzled. "I thought we were meeting here."

We go see my mother, navigating around the beds that are wheeled in and out constantly. Visiting hours are for fifteen minutes every two hours. When we get to her bed, it is empty and I have a horrible sinking feeling. Then I see my mother standing up in a corner of the ER, talking on the only phone in the vicinity. She is wearing a pale green pajama-like outfit. She waves at us.

"She got the only pair of scrubs in the ER," my father says proudly.

My father offers me an eggroll as my mother gets off the phone.

"So girls," says my mother, kissing me and my sister, "what's new?"

"Aren't you supposed to be on a low-salt diet?" I say sternly to my mother.

Both my parents look sheepish.

Back in her bed, my mother sits up and eats lo mein. She is no longer hooked up to the heart monitor. A nurse comes by to take her pulse.

My mother smiles at her. "Hey Annalee, how's it going?"

My mother, of course, has become close with the nurses. She has an amazing ability to be close with strangers.

"You've gotta get your pressure down lower than this, Mrs. Ferber," says the nurse, reading the printout from the machine.

My mother shrugs. "I'll try, see you later." My mother describes the procedures and tests they've given her, clinically, as if she were the doctor. They still haven't found anything wrong, and they still haven't found a bed for her. A doctor comes over and hands her a large green pill.

"What is it?" my mother asks.

He waves his hand around vaguely. "It's complicated."

"I'm a Ph.D., I think I can understand it."

As the doctor explains the medication, a time-release blood pressure drug, my mother takes notes on the back of *The New Yorker* and my sister and I smile at each other. She looks more like her old self and I feel a great weight is being lifted from my chest.

After fifteen minutes, the guard tells us to leave, nicely, recognizing us from before.

We go to the nearest bar, a loud sports bar, and have a drink. My father and I get vodka gimlets and my sister gets a glass of white wine.

Bringing the drinks back to the table, my father spills them a little. My father is handsome in a gray-haired, professorial kind of way. A few weeks ago, a girl in a candy store told him he should be an actor.

"He looks just like that guy on *Dynasty*," she said to me.

"Oh yeah, John Forsythe. I can see it," I said.

My father was embarrassed, yet pleased after I explained what *Dynasty* was.

"Did you tell the guys at tennis—about Mom being sick?" I ask, squeezing a lime into my drink.

"Yes, and it was surprisingly helpful, because Seymour is a doctor and he explained some things to me."

"Good," says Bette.

WE START REMINISCING about places we lived when we were little, a common pastime. Within the family, I am famous for my bad memory. My sister sketches the layout of our Brooklyn house on a napkin, continuing an ongoing family debate about the past, where we lived, for how long.

"I remember a baby gurgling. You," my father says, pointing at Bette, "gurgling in a crib in the closet."

He turns to me, "You know, Liza, babies are very happy when they wake up."

Bette sounds exasperated. "Dad, that couldn't have been me, I was five years old, it must have been Liza."

"You kept me in a closet?" I say, "No wonder I'm screwed up."

"It wasn't a closet exactly," says my father. "At least, it was a walk-in closet."

My sister moves on to the layout of the Washington house on a new cocktail napkin. I can't remember the inside of this house at all, although I lived there from the time I was two until I was five. The outside was white, with huge white pillars, and I used to tell people I lived in the White House. I can remember the yard, my brother forbidding me to take apples from the tree out back. He was mean to me and I adored him. But I still can't remember the inside of the house. When I try to open the door and walk inside there is a void.

"Perhaps you have False Memory Syndrome," says my sister.

"Don't give her ideas." My father smiles.

My sister is determined to make me remember.

"Remember our room, Liza. We shared a room."

"I never shared a room. I would remember that."

"The wrought iron headboards that our hair would always get caught in."

I glimpse a vague memory of pain and my father combing large tangles out of my hair. I run my hand over my now short spiky hair and, for a moment, miss the long messy hair of my childhood.

"You two are hopeless," sighs my sister. "I'll have to ask Mom."

I N THE OFFICE the next day, Stan has transferred his affections to Shoshana, the other young lawyer besides Tad. Everyone tries to explain to him that Shoshana is religious and would never go out with a non-Jew. He is hoping she'll make an exception.

I notice that since Stan's arrival, Roxanne, the receptionist, has taken to wearing sexier clothes, today a tight miniskirt with high heels. I hear them talking about his ex-wife, and her sympathizing.

"Could it be possible," Tad whispers to me in the library, "that she is attracted to him?"

"Well, you heard what she said about her sex life."

Roxanne has confided in us that she doesn't have sex with her husband, or as she puts it, "I don't give him any." Tad and I are shocked by this. I don't know about Tad and his boyfriend, but I frequently want to have sex with Gregor, although we usually confine it to long weekend mornings, because he likes to take his time.

IN THE AFTERNOON, my father calls to update me.

"They found some plaque on an artery, plaque like on your teeth."

"So what does that mean?"

"Well, your mother's mother, your grandmother, had a stroke. You remember."

I shift my phone from ear to ear. "How could I remember, I wasn't even born."

My father laughs, embarrassed. "Oh, I must have been thinking about your sister."

"Does that mean Mommy could have a stroke?"

"No, it's a hereditary possibility. They're not even sure how much plaque there is, they're going to do some more tests, maybe a stress test."

I VISIT MY MOTHER after work, by myself. She has been transferred to the fourteenth floor, to a floor with rooms that are like a luxury hotel compared to the emergency room. I bring her herbal teas and articles on relaxation. She has a TV and a refrigerator. She is sitting on a chair. I try to get her to lie down, but she says she's fine.

My mother confides in me that even before this, unpleasant incidents have been happening for several years, ever since she started thinking about retirement, and especially since the impending demise of the dream program, which was her creation. In the past two years, she has crashed her car, lost her keys six times, and had various stomach problems.

I take her blood pressure with the cuff I bought at Radio Shack. She wants to do it herself but I insist. As I wrap the fabric around her arm gently but securely, I say, "Well, maybe this is a warning, that you need to deal with some of this stuff. I mean, you never even wanted to talk about what was happening with the program, or retiring."

"I guess I didn't want to burden anyone."

After a few tries, I get a normal blood pressure reading.

"So what does the doctor say?"

"Well, everything has come out basically normal, even the plaque, so he is going to release me tomorrow."

"Good."

"He suggested I go into therapy." My mother says this very quietly.

"It's not a bad idea, is it?" For people who are in the help-

ing profession, my parents have always had a particular aver-
sion to going into therapy themselves. I think they see it as a
weakness, something that other people need.

"I have to think about it."

IN THE ELEVATOR going down, I feel too light, and I realize I forgot my pocketbook.

I glide back up to my mother's room.

She opens the door, looking smaller now that I have left.
She is happy that I forgot my bag.

"That shows that you didn't want to go."

I laugh and kiss her good night, feeling closer to her than I
have in many years. My mother seems vulnerable now, and I
feel there is an opening for me to slip into.

THE DAY AFTER my mother gets out of the hospital, I run
into her and my father strolling down Columbus
Avenue, near the apartment they have recently pur-
chased. They bought the apartment, an alcove studio, before
they found out about my mother's forced retirement from
teaching, and now they are intent on furnishing it.

Reading the Help Wanted section of the Sunday paper, I
see them from the window of a coffee bar, their pale faces
pressed up against the other side of the glass.

"I told you that was her," my mother says triumphantly,
beaming at my father, as she lets in a cold blast of air through
the open door. They are carrying a large shopping bag with a
colorful woven thing peeking out.

"Dad, close the door," I hiss. "Mom, you shouldn't be out."

My father looks wounded. "Is that any way to greet us,
daughter?"

"Eliza, I feel absolutely wonderful being out of the hospital, an entirely new person. I have never appreciated wearing clothes so much."

"Mom, I still want you to go to yoga with me."

"Do you want to come up and see the rug we bought?" my father asks. "It's a Kelim."

I shake my head. "No, I have to get going soon."

My parents leave in a rush, as if furnishing their apartment is a task in a game show and each second counts.

After they leave, I sip my cappuccino guiltily, as if I have no right to enjoy myself.

Chapter four

W ATCHING MY SISTER on the podium, in the outfit we spent three hours in Bloomingdales' picking out, a pale blue silk dress with a matching jacket, I have a rush of pride and envy. Bette, shy in real life, is at ease in her area of expertise.

The name of her talk is "Deconstructing Toast." Along with several other well-funded English literature graduate students, she is presenting a paper. They do it elegantly at her university. The talk is held in a mahogany lecture room, the walls lined with books, an unobtrusive podium, a reception afterward. She is discussing the function of toast in British society. Bette seems so confident, so in control. She doesn't use notes like some of the other speakers, just a few overhead images, a pot of Earl Grey tea beside a plate of scones, familiar foods, comfort foods.

The audience probably imagines these are the foods she ate growing up, but the only tea I remember is Lipton's, and I didn't have a personal experience with a scone until I was in my late twenties. My sister cooked for me and my brother

41

when we were growing up. My parents weren't home for dinner much and my sister got sick of eating TV dinners every night. She cooked simple food: spaghetti, pork chops, hamburgers cooked in Kosher salt, and, if we were sad, tuna noodle casserole and brownies for dessert.

When my parents cooked, mostly on weekends, the menu was much more unpredictable. My mother went through periods of food, the phyllo period, long buttery sheets laid out on the rough wooden counters, magically transformed into tiny golden triangles filled with spinach and cheese, or baklava, even phyllo lasagna. Then there was the Chinese period when everything had to be cooked in a wok, the endless chili phase, the Crock-Pot winter.

My mother prided herself on never using recipes. "I cook by instinct," she would say, throwing in garlic by the handful. To this day, I peruse cookbooks with a secret guilty pleasure, as if they are pornographic.

I never cooked growing up, and I rarely cook now, but I did cook when I lived with Charles in San Francisco, Charles the lawyer, who I believed was the love of my life. I took gourmet cooking classes at a tiny school on a steep hill. It was very expensive and it turned out I was mistaken about Charles. I liked cooking but it filled me with anxiety. I wanted to cook the perfect risotto, the Grand Marnier soufflé that would never fall. The class gave me confidence and on the nights of my cooking class I brought home choux pastries chubby with cream, individual portions of rack of lamb, homemade paté. Charles paid for the cooking classes but I was so excited when I came home, so full of liqueur and Belgian chocolate, he would become disconcerted, as if he wasn't sure he wanted me to be that happy away from him. When I brought him my wax paper offerings, he'd say he wasn't hungry, or he was tired, and I would store the risotto or the flourless chocolate torte in our Subzero refrigerator as he rolled away from me on our soft

42

white bed. I would forget about the food until months later, when I was no longer able to identify it.

That apartment was all white, with a Jacuzzi in the bathroom and fourteen-karat gold fixtures, proudly pointed out to us by the spindly real estate agent. It was a chilly apartment though, and I would wander from room to room, wrapping an old sweater around me, never really warm enough.

AFTER MY SISTER'S talk is over, I find myself next to a professor. I introduce myself. He is Professor Boombar, a professor of interdisciplinary studies, one of my sister's advisors. He is tall and gray with a bad case of dandruff.

"So, what do you do?" he says.

I feel compelled to tell the truth.

"I work in a law firm," I say, hating the words as they leave my lips. What I do is so meaningless. My sister's colleagues are all in academia and I envy them. They have jobs they can be proud to answer to at cocktail parties, they have curriculum vitaes, offices, degrees.

"Oh, an attorney, noble profession. At least it once was." He plays with his wineglass, as if he is in a wine-tasting seminar: sniff, swirl, sip, swallow.

"I'm not an attorn—" I am thankfully interrupted by a lanky waiter in a tuxedo who has an affluent air, unlike most of the guests.

"Sushi," he says disdainfully, pushing a highly polished silver tray in our direction.

I grab two pieces that are shaped like igloos and motion my hand toward the bar as I move away from him, murmuring, "Nice to meet you, Professor."

He looks at his tiny igloo of rice wrapped in raw fish sadly, "You'd think they'd have buttered toast, given the subject matter."

I keep thinking about my job. There is nothing I can say to

43

make it sound acceptable. Legal secretary. Legal assistant. Paralegal. What would I want to be? I took a career counseling test once and they said my psychological profile perfectly matched that of an anesthesiologist.

My sister and I were both bookish growing up. We considered it a treat if we got to read at the dinner table when my mother and father were working late. My brother didn't like to read at dinner, but he was usually out smoking pot with his friends or at soccer practice. If my father was there, he'd insist on conversation to improve our minds, but if we were alone, my sister and I would prop our books up on salt shakers and candlesticks and read contentedly, letting our food get cold and the candles burn down into thick waxy pools. We'd go through phases, only reading gothic novels, or mysteries, or romances. One year, my sister got into a nineteenth-century British period and she has yet to emerge.

After my sister went off to college in upstate New York, I started reading biographies, biographies about depressed people, psychotic people, suicidal people. I read *I Never Promised You a Rose Garden* five times and decided I was destined for a future in psychology. On my one and only college interview, at Clark University, they showed me the chair Freud had sat in during his brief lecture tour in the United States.

"Clark University was founded as the first nondenominational graduate school in the United States," the admissions representative told me, fondling the faded red velvet of the Freud chair, "and it is expressly written into our charter that there can be no fraternities or sororities, no football team."

I knew this was the school for me, no group activities, no school spirit. I didn't even have to write an essay in my application. I submitted an old behavioral science paper on multiple personalities and got accepted early admission, before I had too much time to think about it.

College wasn't what I expected. It centered around beer,

the smell of which made me nauseous, and socializing in the library. I would hide in a corner carrel, my hiking boots propped up on the desk, eating cheese and reading Oscar Wilde plays.

In statistics class, I played dots with my friend Don in the back row, peering down at our fiercely scribbling classmates below, baffled by the concept of analysis of variance. I got a D and decided I wasn't cut out for psychology, a decision that was echoed by the professors at Clark who informed the undergraduate pysch majors that the vast majority of us wouldn't get into doctoral programs, especially at Clark, even if we applied.

I GO UP to my sister and hand her a glass of wine. "Your paper was great, I especially liked the part about butter and love."

"Do you think that made sense, about garlic and social pressure?"

"Yes, I love that, what book is that from?"

"*Jane and Prudence.* Jane says, 'I should have liked the kind of life where one ate food flavored with garlic, but it was not to be.' I'm thinking on using that for a lecture on condiments for the Barbara Pym Society."

"They'll love it. By the way, the dress looks great. Hey, who is that cute guy over by the French literature crowd?"

"Oh, that's Jake, another graduate student, he's doing Celtic folktales."

"Well?" I ask. "What's wrong with him?"

"Nothing. Liza, don't start with me. Listen, I've got to go talk to my advisor. Do you want to wait for me? We'll get a drink after."

"All right."

MY SISTER IS trapped in a tower, the victim of an evil spell. She rises in the morning, she does her research, she runs around the Jackie Kennedy Onassis Reservoir, but she has lost the will to desire. She reads in her solitary tower, but she keeps herself at a distance, even from me.

She is not unemotional. If I bring up the subject of her ex, she starts to cry, unwillingly, as if it's some kind of weakness.

"Don't you ever wonder about him?" I asked her the other night.

"No," she said, dabbing her eyes with a Kleenex, as tears streamed down her face.

"Look, I just think you need to figure out what happened before you can move on."

After these conversations, I feel guilty, mean. Bette is not some poor pathetic person. She has a career, a nice apartment. She reads a lot of books, goes to museums, is up on current events. But I am afraid she is going to become one of those characters in the novels she writes about. Someone going home at night to their solitary apartment, getting comfort from a single soft-boiled egg and a nice cup of tea.

WHEN MY SISTER got divorced, my parents were devastated. They kept asking me, "But what was the real reason?" It was as though they thought I knew the deep dark secret, as if I would say to them one day, "Oh, Tom was really an alien and he had to go back to the home world."

There was no clear reason, except that Tom was feeling dissatisfied with his life, and Bette found a pair of black thong underwear in her bed, something so far from what she would ever wear as to be doubly insulting. You'd think that infidelity would be enough of a reason for my parents to rally to my sister's side, crying out to the world, "That no-good Tom!" but they just worried about her single state and quizzed me periodically: "Come on, that couldn't be the only reason, there must be more."

When my sister and Tom split up, she said she was fine. When she stopped being fine, she agreed to go into therapy, at my prodding. Therapy is a big deal for my sister. She has never considered herself the kind of person who would ever need it, and at first, she was kind of ashamed about going. When I was in college, I remember her saying to me that she had never been depressed, although she was very sympathetic when I was, which was frequently. I have been to a number of therapists: the good, the bad, the indifferent. The first time I went was in my sophomore year in college when I refused to get out of bed, drinking wine from a jug and sleeping through all my classes. After a couple of weeks, my friend Don called a psych graduate student he was sleeping with who agreed to make a house call. The graduate student was short and chubby but had kind blue eyes. The minute he arrived, I started crying. Don made hors d'oeuvres as if we were at a cocktail party, then left us alone, and soon I started to feel better, maybe from the attention.

My sister's psychiatrist gave her a diagnosis. "Social phobia," she told me, sounding pleased, as if it's not her fault. My sister's psychiatrist believes her fears stem from a chemical imbalance, a genetic mishap. According to her, our parents are merely witnesses, not perpetrators.

I LOOK AROUND for my sister, the social phobic, who is probably happily chatting away to someone about the role of domestics in Thomas Hardy novels. I like literature, too, but dissecting it seems cruel to me, an inhumane treatment of books.

I spot the cute graduate student, the one I want for my sister, over by the stained-glass window, and I maneuver myself next to where he is standing. I fiddle with my wineglass, practically bumping into him.

He turns to me, holding out his hand. "You must be Bette's sister. I'm Jake."

We shake hands. He has very dark hair and manners out of a Jane Austen novel. I wish I had a dissertation to discuss.

We talk for a few minutes and he doesn't ask what I do, which I am grateful for. I try to recall anything I might know about Celtic myths but all that comes to mind is a picture of a large blond god looming out from a picture book I had as a child. I describe it.

"No, that's Thor," he tells me politely. "Norse, not my thing at all."

"Listen, I seem to have lost my sister, would you help me find her?"

"Sure," he says, and we navigate our way through the crowd. My sister is talking to an Anita Brookner scholar about sentence structure and they say hi to us, but keep on talking.

"So," I ask Jake, feeling like a Jewish mother, "you live in the City?"

"Yes, downtown, although I'm originally from Scotland."

I glance down at his hands but I don't see a ring. "Really!"

"I've moved here recently. I'm on a fellowship you see. And where do you live, Liza?"

"Oh, on the Upper East Side, near Bette, as a matter of fact."

I hear Bette saying good-bye to the Anita Brookner lady. She turns to Jake. "So what did you think of my whole Jungian tangent, was it too much?"

"No, not at all. I think you're right about the warrior archetype being expressed in the women, especially in that scene where they're fighting over rock cakes at the jumble sale."

"No more shoptalk," I groan. "Can't we talk about TV or something?"

Jake and my sister smile at each other as he leaves and I see a vision of them in their country cottage in England, drinking tea and writing articles across an antique wooden table littered with crumbs from breakfast.

M Y SISTER AND I go to an English pub in our neighborhood. She drinks stout and I have a vodka gimlet straight up.

"You should ask him out."

My sister looks at me incredulously. "You know I have social phobia."

"You seemed to be doing fine at the lecture."

"Well, that's work, the phobia only manifests in situations where intimacy is a possibility."

"Intimacy is always a possibility."

"Anyway, it's a moot point, because he has a girlfriend—feminist studies, she's very nice. By the way, have you heard from the parental units?"

"Nice change of subject. Yes. We've been invited for Passover at Aunt Minnie's. We're supposed to bring the wine. Did I tell you that the day after Mommy got out of the hospital, I saw them on Columbus Avenue buying a rug?"

My sister shakes her head at their folly.

"A Kelim, and they wanted me to go up and look at it."

"I can top that. Do you know that on the way home from the hospital, they stopped to buy plates for the new apartment?"

"God forbid they shouldn't be well equipped when Mommy has another attack."

I take a long sip of my drink, "When I saw them, I told her she should go right to bed."

"They never listen."

"I know. Listen, Bette, do you ever think about the fact that our names are the names of loud entertainers that are worshipped by gay men—Bette Midler and Liza Minnelli?"

"Well, you're really E-liza, like Eliza Doolittle, and I refuse to be Bette Midler. I'd rather be Bette Davis, even though she pronounces it Betty."

"Okay, you can be Bette Davis and I'll be Eliza Doolittle, after she's learned how to talk properly."

We clink our glasses. "Cheers."

Chapter five

THERE ARE TWO holidays this weekend, Passover and Easter. For a nonreligious person, it seems excessive that I am going to both, first Passover with my family, then Easter with Gregor's. Gregor was a big hit at last year's seder and this year he is actually looking forward to going. He likes gefilte fish and brisket and all those bland, heavy Jewish foods. I submit to going but my sister has to be practically dragged.

"I'm very busy," she says, "working on my dissertation."

"You know that's not going to work. Face it, you can't get out of it. Me, I'm resigned."

"You say that because you have Gregor. Having the boyfriend takes the pressure off."

"You should try it." My sister makes a noise.

WE DO NOT have a traditional Passover ceremony. As I try to explain to the guys in my neighborhood liquor store, I don't have to get kosher wine. They miss the point. "But there are some very good kosher wines. People buy them all year round."

51

I don't want to offend them, so I buy a Baron Herzog chardonnay, which has only been touched by kosher hands, at least until it is opened by me at the seder. I try to picture a Jewish baron, a suave guy on a horse with a silky black yarmulke on his head.

AT THE SEDER, Gregor sings folk songs with my aunt, who plays the guitar. I eat massive amounts of potato kugel, and throughout the course of the evening my sister and I polish off all the Baron Herzog chardonnay.

WHILE WE'RE SITTING at the table waiting for the matzo ball soup, my father uses this opportunity to ask me how my life is going.

"How's it going, really?" he asks confidentially.

I tell him I am seeing a therapist. "I'm trying to figure out what to do with my life."

"What's his training?"

"Her," I say, starting to feel uncomfortable. "I don't know, I lie on the couch, so I guess it's analytical."

"What's her name, maybe I know her."

"Dad!"

"Do you find it helpful?"

I nod.

"Well, as long as you don't become one of those people who go forever."

"Don't worry, I couldn't afford it."

"And, Gregor, things are going well?"

My parents believe that if we are in a relationship, everything is fine. If we aren't, they worry.

"Yeah, I guess so. I told you he doesn't want to live together or anything."

"Well, don't pressure him. And your job?"

"Well, you know." I hesitate before telling him that I am

52

thinking of looking for another job. When I first started working as a legal secretary, my father asked me, "How can you sit there and type all day?" I wondered the same thing myself, but I didn't want to hear it from him.

Now I say, "I might look around, see what's out there."

My father looks concerned and pleased. He takes some horseradish off the platter and puts it on a boiled egg, popping it into his mouth neatly.

"Yes, you ought to get out soon, before it's too late. You are thirty-two after all."

I sip some of the Baron's chardonnay and try not to look upset. I hear the words *too late too late*, booming in my head. Is it too late? Am I really stuck in this job forever, bringing Darla bacon cheeseburgers and milk shakes for the rest of my life?

I change the subject and ask about my brother, who manages to escape all the holidays by living in Central America.

"He wanted to come, but he has too many patients that rely on him."

"What's he into these days?"

"He's doing some kind of energy healing, Rake or something."

"I think that's Reiki, Dad."

GREGOR IS TALKING to my cousin Arnold about computers on the other side of the table. I want him to rescue me but he doesn't even look over. A young relative is toasting a piece of matzo over one of the candles. I try to dissect a huge matzo ball into edible pieces. A woman someone brought is talking about vision quests, and I look at my sister and roll my eyes. I hear the woman say, "Peyote, but it's not like taking drugs."

OVER THE POT roast and potato pancakes, a discussion circles around our end of the table about which organization had more FBI informants, the Communist Party or the Black Panthers.

"It was definitely the party," says my father, gesturing with a pickle. "Every other member was practically an informant. I remember one time we all thought this guy Hymie was one, and no one would talk to him."

"Was he?" says Bette, leaning forward eagerly.

"As it turned out he wasn't, but everyone still avoided him anyway."

"That's mean," I say.

My father shrugs.

"Remember those classes we used to have to take?" my father asks, looking over at my mother.

"Yes," she says, lowering her eyes, as if recalling an intimate moment. "They were always talking about the concept of surplus value."

"What's surplus value?" asks my young cousin.

"It's when a worker makes more than he can consume," my mother says briskly, stacking plates together in a noisy pile.

"Right," I say, as if I knew it all the time.

AFTER DINNER, I make coffee in the kitchen. My mother sits down at the kitchen table and asks me about Gregor.

"So what's going on. Are you two getting serious?"

"Well . . ." I say, putting cinnamon in the coffee grounds.

As I pour in the water, my mother starts telling me a story about this man she almost married before she married my father. She decided she couldn't marry him at a Chinese restaurant because he didn't leave enough money for the tip.

"I had been a waitress in the Catskills and one thing I knew about was tipping."

While my mother is talking I start to feel insubstantial, as if the act of thinking about her marrying another man could unwrite history and I would begin to dematerialize.

I recall that my mother has told me a similar story, except it was to illustrate a different point. In the earlier story, she was engaged to a man before she met my father, but she realized she couldn't marry him after they had slept together. She told me this the day after I slept with Kenny Goldstein, while I was pacing around the house, waiting for him to call me.

WHEN I TOLD her it was my first time, my mother said, "I thought you did that a long time ago."

MY AUNT BRINGS out Italian cookies and cakes, and a honeycomb made up of balls of gooey pastry. I take a miniature Italian cheesecake. Gregor comes over and he and my father take pastry blobs off the pyramid. They have similar tastes in food. This scares me. It is too late for me, and my boyfriend and my father may be the same person.

Before we leave, my father corners my sister over by the piano. He waves a piece of matzo at her.

"So Bet, how long have you been living in the City, it must be three or four years now."

"I think so."

"And in all that time, have you gone out on a date?" My father sounds annoyed, as if my sister is holding out on him, depriving him of the pleasure of her dating.

I rush over to where my sister is standing. She doesn't say anything, just stares at my father, as if she's been struck.

"Dad, stop torturing her!" I say.

"I wasn't torturing her, I was asking her a simple question, you girls are so sensitive." He walks away, shaking his head, as if he is the wounded party.

Y FATHER DRIVES us back into New York, through bad neighborhoods to avoid paying a toll. My mother doesn't want him to drive us. "They'll be fine," she says. "They can take the train."

We're not worried, we know he will drive us. That is how my father shows affection, by driving us places. We could always count on him to pick us up at the airport, drive us to the train, drive for hours to show us colleges. Now my father takes a shortcut through a bad neighborhood, and I worry about him driving back alone through the deserted burned-out streets. What if the car broke down? My sister and I make him promise to drive back on the highway. He says, "Okay," as if to indulge us, but we know he won't follow our advice.

When we get out of the car, my sister says to me, "Now you know why I never tell them anything."

T IS EASTER Sunday. Today, we are going to see Gregor's parents, and, like most other people's parents, they frighten me. They don't speak out on any topic that pops into their heads. They are more restrained. Manners were never a prerequisite in my house, only ideas, while in other people's houses manners are essential and ideas are suspect.

I remember the time I came home from a friend's house and told my mother that we were supposed to put napkins in our laps, not just have them on the table. I felt cheated. "Why didn't you tell me?"

My mother sighed deeply as though I'd disappointed her, "Eliza, just because everyone else does it doesn't mean we have to. Look, if you need a napkin you can use one. You know where they are. There's no reason for it to be on your lap."

I GO OVER to Gregor's apartment. We are supposed to meet at twelve. I get there early, at eleven-thirty. There is a note taped to the door of his building. He'll be late. I go inside to the elevator. There is another note taped to the elevator door saying that the elevator will be out of order for a week. I trudge up the five flights of stairs, throw my things down on Gregor's bed. I wonder if I have worn the right thing.

I sit on his old couch, picking at a pillow. I critique his apartment in my head. I wouldn't want to live here anyway. I throw his note to me in the garbage. When we were first going out, I kept all the notes I got from him as if they were archeological treasures, to be preserved and periodically analyzed.

After a while, I hear Gregor's key in the lock and I stiffen. I want to be mad at him but I'm glad he's here.

"Where were you?" I feel as if I haven't seen him for weeks, not two days.

He is carrying flowers.

"I had some things to do, I got some flowers for my mother. How long have you been here?"

"Forever. I got here early."

"Well that's not my fault." He hands me something. It's a tiny basket filled with little pastel eggs and tiny chocolates.

I start crying and he comes over and hugs me.

He says, "You're crazy, you know that, nuts."

"HAPPY PASSOVER," SAYS Gregor's mother. She is wearing a flowered dress and stockings. I am glad I have worn a dress, although it is black, not pastel.

"Happy Easter," I say. I have brought chocolates in the shape of Easter bunnies.

Gregor's parents have made lasagna for Easter.

57

He whispers to me, "I told them you could eat anything, that you weren't kosher, but they insisted."

We eat nonstop from the time of arrival, potato chips and dip, cheese and crackers, chocolate. I gulp glasses of wine, I eat two pieces of lasagna. I imagine the glistening ham that they would be carving if I weren't there.

There are silences at dinner, silences that make me uncomfortable. I want to fill them in. They are like the silences while I am waiting for my therapist to say something.

Gregor's family doesn't ask him about his acting. They don't approve. After seeing him in his first showcase at the acting school, his father said he didn't think Gregor had much natural talent. Now they just don't talk about it.

GREGOR'S MOTHER STARTS to clear the dishes. No one moves. I hesitate. Should I get up and help? I never know what is expected of me. I grab a few dishes and walk into the kitchen. All the counter space is full, so I stand near the garbage, holding the delicate plates awkwardly. I want to ask Gregor's mother where she wants me to put the dishes but I never know what to call her. Mrs. Roberts? Camille? Gregor's mother? Finally, I stack the plates precariously on top of some other dishes and go back to my seat.

His mother brings out dessert, a strawberry rhubarb pie smothered in cream. They drink tea. I am the only one who takes it with milk and sugar. They bring me out my own sugar dish and creamer. I try to have manners, not spill food or say anything inappropriate. I make a point not to talk about politics.

After dinner, Gregor and his father study the figures from their mutual funds in the living room.

Gregor's mother tells me about Gregor's uncle, who was a bachelor for his entire life.

"Gregor's just like him."

I smile, trying to think calm thoughts.

Sitting on the puffy couch after dinner, I realize the problem with Christian holidays. Unless you go to church there are no activities but sitting around and eating and drinking. At least at the seder, we have to read from the Haggadah, make the children answer questions, hide the matzo.

As I ponder possible Catholic games (hide the wafer or wise men's bluff?), Gregor's father comes into the living room with a big smile. He hands me a box.

"It's macaroons," he says, "certified by the Rabbi."

I smile and take one.

Gregor looks exasperated. "But you hate coconut," he whispers.

"No, I don't," I say, as well as I can while choking down the dusty, dry yet sickeningly sweet piece of cookie. "Thank you."

"They're real kosher," Gregor's father tells me. "You can take them with you."

GREGOR AND I are exhausted by the time we get back to New York, but we are relieved to be home, far from suburbia. Too stuffed to eat our chocolate bunnies, we fizz up some Alka-Seltzers and roll around on the bed, trying to get comfortable.

"I think your parents liked me more this time," I tell Gregor, as we are drifting off to sleep.

"What's not to like?" says Gregor, in his version of a Yiddish accent.

I turn to say something else to him, but he is already asleep.

Chapter Six

IT'S RAINING AND Bette and I are on our way to Queens to visit Mrs. Lumpkin, the famous Jewish matchmaker. We travel on the subway through unfamiliar urban landscapes, squirming on our molded plastic seats.

My sister looks as if we are on a field trip to the dentist. "I can't believe we're doing this," she moans.

"Well, maybe it will be amusing," I say, trying to be optimistic.

The only way my sister's analyst has been able to nudge her into action is by giving her assignments. Every week she has to do something toward meeting someone. This week it's Mrs. Lumpkin. Apparently the matchmaker works for free, for the sheer pleasure of bringing people together.

"It's exactly like that movie with Amy Irving," I say, "where they fix her up with the Jewish pickle guy, and she doesn't realize how great he is."

"I've never even dated a Jewish guy. They're so . . ."

"Familiar. I know, but they're supposed to make the best husbands."

"Why should I take your advice? What about Gregor? He's not Jewish."

"Okay, I haven't dated any Jewish guys lately, but I'm not against it. Hey, what about Kenny Goldstein?"

"That was in high school. Look, maybe I need to go home. I have a lot of work to do."

"You can analyze crumpets tomorrow, this is important."

MRS. LUMPKIN LIVES in an unprepossessing brownstone in Forest Hills, not far from the train station.

She is pleased to see us. "Sisters, this is good," she says. "Who is the oldest? No, don't tell me, you." She points a chubby finger at me.

"No, she's the oldest," I say irritably.

Bette smiles happily.

MRS. LUMPKIN GIVES us Russian tea in tall glasses with small plates of raspberry jam.

"Thank you," says Bette politely, taking a small spoonful of jam and stirring it into her tea, in a precise imitation of Mrs. Lumpkin.

I do the same.

MRS. LUMPKIN HAS a large white appliqué kitten on her sweater. I keep staring at it.

"So, who is the lucky girl, the girl who wants to meet someone?" she says loudly in a strong Yiddish accent. My sister sips her tea. I nudge my head in her direction.

"It's her. I have a boyfriend."

"Oh, your sister, a lovely girl, I have some ideas already. How old are you, thirtyish, no need to say exactly. We've got some beautiful boys here. If you follow my advice I have you under a *chuppa* in no time," Mrs. Lumpkin proclaims in her thick Yiddish accent, walking out of the room.

My sister looks baffled.

"You know," I whisper, "a *chuppa*, that thing they stand under at Jewish weddings."

"Right, a *chuppa*. How do you know so much about all this, anyway?"

"There's a religious attorney in my office. She's trying to bring me back into the fold."

Mrs. Lumpkin comes in with a small black case. She unzips it and pulls out a small laptop computer.

"So what are we looking for—height, location, income?"

I speak to Mrs. Lumpkin over Bette's silent head. "You know, smart, good-looking, witty."

Mrs. Lumpkin punches in a few numbers. "You want to meet someone, I got someone beautiful here for you, five-ten, a doctor."

"What kind of a doctor?" I ask.

"A dermatologist, no emergencies."

My sister and I touch our faces self-consciously.

"No doctors," I say, and I see Bette shaking her head also. "Too self-involved."

"No problem. Here, I got another one. A scientist."

She tilts the screen in our direction and a face composed of tiny dots appears. A nice face, not gorgeous but a nice face.

My sister looks at it impassively.

"He could be your *bashert*," says Mrs. Lumpkin knowingly.

"My what?"

"Your soul mate," I translate. "Anyway, what have you got to lose?"

"I'll e-mail him tomorrow," says Mrs. Lumpkin, shutting her computer off with a definitive click. "Oh, by the way, Steve, his name is Steve."

*T*HE NEXT DAY, Steve calls my sister.

"He sounds okay," Bette tells me grudgingly.

"Look, it'll be fine, there's no obligation, you just go out and have a good time."

"He's a meteorologist."

"Is that good or bad?"

"I'm not sure."

"So, what are you going to do?"

"Dinner and a movie."

"Wardrobe?"

"We'll have to discuss it."

"I think something simple, yet elegant—black."

"Liza, all you ever wear is black."

"That way I'm always coordinated. I never have to worry about my shoes."

*T*HE NIGHT OF the date, I am even more nervous than Bette is. I go over and hang out with her while she gets ready. I watch her put on the outfit she is going to wear, a blue chenille sweater and a flowing skirt.

"You look very nice," I say, sipping my martini. "Put on these earrings, the long silver ones."

"I should be the one having the drink."

"No, you are too calm. You know if this works out, maybe I should quit my job and become a matchmaker, that would be a satisfying profession. I could apprentice with Mrs. Lumpkin, get my own laptop."

"Let's see what happens, I don't even know if I like him."

"Call me later and tell me how it went—or call me at Gregor's if I'm not home. Or I'll call you tomorrow. Except what if . . ."

"What?"

"You know . . ." I raise my eyebrows suggestively.

"That's not going to happen."

"I was kidding."

REGOR AND I stay in, at his apartment. I feel restless. We watch a bad movie about a dissatisfied couple in London trying to sell a Henry Moore statue and I wonder if we're a dissatisfied couple in New York. After the movie, the news comes on, flooding the room with bombings, killings, and natural disasters. I feel as if they are all happening to me.

Gregor nudges me. "Are you okay? I'm going to make some tea, you want some?"

"Everything seems so depressing. Chamomile please. I wonder how the date is going."

Gregor gives me my tea. "Do you wish you were going out on a date?"

"A date? What do you mean a date? With someone else?"

I try to imagine it for a moment, the white tablecloth, the awkward conversation, the wine, but Gregor's face keeps appearing on the other side of my table.

"Don't be silly. If I wanted to go out on a date, I'd want to go on it with you."

"Well if it's okay with your date, it's okay with me."

I punch him softly with a pillow.

"Stop, seriously. How about it? Tomorrow night, we'll have our own date."

I CALL MY sister in the morning.

"Hi, so?"

"Well, I don't think he's my type. He Rollerblades and he's kind of religious."

"Oh well, but the important thing is that you went."

"You know I'm kind of relieved, I think I'm more afraid of something working out than not working out."

"What's so bad about things working out?"

"I don't know, I guess I'm afraid of feeling trapped."

"Were you before, with Tom?"

"I guess I was."

"Well, maybe it doesn't have to be like that."

"Maybe." Bette sounds unconvinced.

GREGOR AND I go to our favorite Indian restaurant for our date.

He looks very handsome in his white poet's shirt and black pants. I don't want him going on dates with anyone else.

As the waiter ceremoniously deposits our platters, I can't help myself from blurting out, "You know my lease is coming up in a couple of months."

Gregor carefully arranges some fried onions on his piece of chicken tandoori. He likes to eat all his food together on his fork, a little chicken, a little yogurt, a little rice, a little chutney.

"I know," he says calmly.

"That's it? You know? That's all you're going to say about it?"

He sounds exasperated. "What do you want, Liza?"

"What do I want?" The words explode out of me. "I want to be with you every night. I want to have all my clothes in

66

one place. I want to wake up and have you there beside me. That's what I want."

There is a long silence. We stare at each other and I feel afraid.

Then Gregor says, "Okay."

I pull a piece of paratha bread apart into tiny pieces. "Okay? What do you mean 'Okay'?"

"I mean, you can move in, in my apartment, we can, you know, live together."

I stare at him, trying to fathom what happened to change his mind, if he has really changed his mind. I remember our last conversation on the subject. It was a disaster.

I kept asking him to explain.

"What is it, is it that you want to see other people?"

"No."

"Is it that you think you will want to see other people in the future?"

"No, that's not it."

"Then why won't you?"

"I don't know, I can't."

We were sitting on his old plaid couch and the moment he said he didn't want to live with me, I couldn't hear anything else. He kept talking and trying to explain but I just curled up into the tiniest, furthest corner of the couch, feeling a familiar sense of abandonment. I felt totally alone. When Gregor reached for my hand, I pulled away. I was already broken up with, already alone in my studio apartment, missing him. Pre-sad.

At the end of the conversation, Gregor said he'd think about it, but I knew it was hopeless. He'd never change his mind. He wanted his freedom. Fine. Since then, I had stopped bringing up the subject.

Now, he smiles at me, and I realize he must have been thinking about us living together for months, cautiously edging himself toward this precipice of cohabitation.

"So are you happy now?" he asks me gruffly.

"Yes. I'm happy."

He looks around the Indian Oven as if it's his living room. "You're not going to start moving things around, are you?"

"No," I laugh. "I tell you what, I won't touch anything."

"Good."

GREGOR IS TRYING out for a play. It's one of those drawing-room comedies I read in college while avoiding classes. All week he has been reading the play, slowly and carefully, practicing his British accent from a tape. I want him to get the part but the more involved he gets in acting, the more I feel this hole at the center of my life where my career is supposed to go.

The day I move in is the day of Gregor's audition. He wears a tuxedo shirt, a bow tie, and highly polished shoes.

"Good luck."

"Are you okay here?"

I nod.

Once the movers and Gregor leave, and all my belongings are scattered around his apartment, I am possessed with a manic energy. I start to unpack everything, every dish, every cup, every plate. I clean all my mirrors with Windex, the full-length mirror, the one on my dresser, the one in the bathroom. I fill the dresser with clothes. I fold each item. I clean the wood on my desk. I want everything to be perfect. I am exhausted but I can't stop unpacking. I have to finish.

As I am starting to unpack my books, Gregor comes back with take-out chicken and tells me to stop. I leave everything where it is, like Pompeii. We clear a place in front of the TV and eat the barbecued chicken and the creamed spinach and the mashed potatoes that come with it. The take-out chicken is the most delicious thing I have ever tasted.

"How was the audition?" I ask.

Gregor gets up and demonstrates his butler stance, the way he holds a tray, his British accent.

"At your service."

"You got it. That's great. You're going to be the best butler ever."

"Thank you m'lady." He bows down low and kisses my hand.

IN THE MIDDLE of the night, I hobble to the bathroom, my calves clenched tight from going up and down the four flights of my walk-up with the movers.

"Where were you?" says Gregor sleepily.

"Nowhere," I whisper, sinking into the warm sleepiness of his body.

Chapter

Seven

GREGOR COMES IN after I've gone to bed. I hear his key in the lock and wait for him to creep into the bedroom. Gregor and I haven't had sex in two weeks. I feel like I am becoming the stereotypical guy in this relationship, always wanting sex. At work, Roxanne used to tell me about her husband "asking for it," and how, most of the time, she refused him. Now I sympathize with husbands everywhere, as I circle my hand around Gregor's sleepy penis, wanting him to respond. He kisses me, and promises we'll have sex on Sunday.

I have dreams, sexual dreams, dreams where all the men I have slept with swirl around me, changing into each other, faces, hands and bodies melting into each other. Charles appears a lot, sometimes Gregor, sometimes Kenny Goldstein from high school.

Except the dreams are never consummated. I keep trying, but the men swirl around me, kissing, touching, teasing. The alarm wakes me up from one of these dreams and I press my body against Gregor who sleeps heavily, moaning softly, as if he is having his own erotic dream. I run my hands over his

71

warm skin, and he wakes for a moment, smiling, as if he is surprised yet pleased to find me beside him.

I imagined when I moved in with Gregor that all my problems would melt away. I thought the same way when I graduated from college, imagining a job would magically appear. Now, I wake up next to Gregor every morning, and at night he makes me chamomile tea, but I am still the same person, aimless, unfocused, waiting for something to happen.

Before he started rehearsal for his current play, he asked me to be understanding.

"Liza, this is going to be a difficult couple of months."

At the time, I was full of understanding, but as the weeks of late rehearsals drag on, I'm starting to feel that I got what I wanted but it's not how I thought it would be.

EVERY DAY, IT is more and more impossible to get up to go to work. I climb under the covers and sleep for the extra five minutes that is the difference between being late and being on time. I've gotten off track, but I don't know how to get back to that point where something else is possible. I look at other people and they seem to possess some secret knowledge I don't have access to. My best friend from high school grew up to be a doctor but none of the jobs I've had since college have led to anything but boredom and anxiety. I knew on the first day of each job that it wasn't going to work. In the morning of each first day, sitting down at each new desk, I would be excited, hopeful. This one would be different, I would tell myself, arranging my new pens around my new stapler and tape dispenser. But by the afternoon, I knew it was hopeless.

IT'S MONDAY, I'M tired, and everything feels like the last straw. Getting coffee for a meeting. The coffee is hazelnut and as I pour it, the sweet smell makes me feel slightly nauseated. What am I doing getting coffee for a meeting? If I had wanted to work as a waitress, I'd work as a waitress. I'm thirty-two years old and getting coffee for a meeting and I'm worried whether or not I should use a coaster. I set the coffee down a little too hard on the marble conference table and walk quickly back to my desk.

"So how's life now that you've tightened the ball and chain?" calls out Tad, as I pass by his office. I immediately regret having told him I moved in with Gregor. I was going to keep it a secret for as long as possible but Tad has a way of getting things out of me.

"Feeling a little hostile this morning, Tad," I retort.

Tad gives me a wounded look, as if I've hurt him, and hands me a form. The law firm is so small that Tad is our benefits plan administrator and I have to decide if I want to participate in the 401(k) plan. Tad's been urging me to get into it since I took the job. The permanence of it frightens me, knowing that year after year, I will get my quarterly statements until I am too feeble to contribute and have to start withdrawing.

"Hey, Tad, how much do you think I should put in?"

"What's your salary?"

I type in a number on his calculator and tilt it toward him.

He laughs. "That's less than what I get taken out in income tax."

"I can't believe you said that."

"Liza, can't you take a joke?"

"It's not funny."

MY ANALYST SAYS we seek out situations that are familiar to us, that the unconscious always knows. It is true that I took this job immediately, the morning of my first interview, not even going to the other two interviews that had already been set up by the employment agency. But Darla spoke so softly, so warmly in the interview, and there were windows that opened and free Snapples in the kitchen.

IN THE AFTERNOON, the plant guys come and leave large trees on the terrace. After they leave, Darla comes out and spies some dirt on her Turkish carpet. She nudges it with her foot. For a large woman she has surprisingly delicate feet. She always wears expensive Italian pumps.

"Eliza, come here and look at this. Did Helmut leave this?"

I stare at the rich reds and blues of the carpet. "I guess."

"Listen, I have a meeting in an hour. Can you do me a huge favor and just run the vacuum over this?"

Although no one in the office ever refuses Darla anything, something deep inside me protests, "No, I don't think . . ."

Darla has already started dragging the vacuum cleaner out of a closet.

"Won't the cleaning people . . ." I start to ask, but she interrupts me, grunting with the effort of lifting the heavy vacuum out of the closet.

"No, by then it will be ground in and I'll never get it out. That's not acceptable." The vacuum cleaner is an ancient stand-up Hoover and when she flicks the on switch it sounds like a plane taking off.

She pushes the vacuum cleaner into my arms and I shove the vacuum cleaner back at her.

"No."

"Eliza, you don't have a choice here. Sometimes we all have to do things we don't want to."

"No."

Darla stares at me, holding the vacuum cleaner in her hands like a reluctant dance partner.

I don't stay to hear her response. I don't care what her

response is. I know I have to leave. I can't do this. I have to leave. *Right away.* Luckily, the other secretaries are in the back so no one sees me or tries to stop me. I grab my jacket from the closet and run out the door, waving my hand at Roxanne, the receptionist, who is answering a call. She calls after me, "Hey Liza, do you know that you used my cup in the meeting?"

I TAKE A cab home. I'm not sure how I feel. In Gregor's apartment, my new apartment, I call my sister.

"Eliza I can't understand a word you're saying. Are you okay? Where are you?"

I pause until I can speak.

"Bette, it was awful."

"What?"

"She made me vacuum and I left. Walked out the door."

"They made you what?"

"Vacuum, but I wouldn't do it."

"Good for you."

"I'm not going back there."

"You don't have to. I still don't understand, how could they make you vacuum! It's absurd."

"I guess I should tell them I'm not coming back."

"Look, why don't you come over and we'll write a formal letter of resignation."

I AM EATING MY second Welsh rarebit at my sister's apartment.

She makes me Earl Grey tea, hot and sweet, the best remedy for an emotional shock.

I start to feel better. We watch daytime TV, an indulgence Bette won't allow herself when she is alone. We watch a talk show about strippers and their boyfriends.

75

"I can't believe that this happened. What am I going to do? Maybe I should be a stripper. At least it's an interesting profession."

"Well they probably wouldn't ask you to vacuum."

All of a sudden I realize what the receptionist's cup said on it: I HAVE PMS AND ESP. WHAT DOES THAT MAKE ME? A BITCH WHO KNOWS IT ALL. I imagine the somber lawyer I gave the cup to turning it around slowly in the meeting and reading the inscription and I start to laugh. I laugh so hard my sister has to hit me on the back to keep me from choking.

Over another cup of tea, my sister says softly, "So Liza, what do you think you want to do now?"

"I would like, for once, to have a job I could be proud of, one that I'd want to go to in the morning. Do you think that's possible?"

"Of course it is."

"I was always so envious of you and your career."

"It's not so great. Sometimes, I feel like I've spent my whole life in school. Believe me, I wouldn't mind a few months off."

I can't believe my sister's nonchalance about her career. What about all those women in all those novels drinking their lonely cups of weak tea? How can she abandon them?

*L*ATE IN THE afternoon, I page Gregor. I'm worried that he will say I shouldn't have quit.

He calls me back a few minutes later. Once he realizes it's an accomplished fact, he says I did the right thing.

"You know, I think you have a good case for unemployment. They shouldn't get away with treating you like that."

"Yeah, why?"

"Well, because vacuuming certainly isn't in your job description."

"But she didn't fire me, I quit."

"Still, I think you should try it. You could take some time off."

"And fall into a deep depression?"

"Not necessarily."

WHY DO I believe I can't have what I want? When I graduated college, I wanted to be in publishing. I liked books, thought it would be perfect. But due to a miscommunication at the employment agency, my first job was in a legal publishing company. During the interview it didn't really hit me, and by the time I took the job it was too late. I typed manuscripts all day long, dull legal manuscripts, until I fell in love with a fellow editorial assistant and got distracted. Andy was older and had written a novel, which seemed incredibly glamorous to me. But once I realized it was legal publishing, why didn't I leave? I could have quit, gotten another job, but I didn't. I felt it was my mistake and I had to live with it.

WALKING THROUGH THE double doors of the employment agency, I feel as if I am plunging into an abyss. I bite my nails in the waiting room, watching the two anorexic receptionists ignore me as they discuss their dance auditions and their boyfriends and their CD collections. They are ballerinas and I hate them. They shove a clipboard at me as I try to hike up my tights, which are slipping ominously downward. I sit down in an uncomfortable chair, my skirt digging into my waist, my coffee cup dribbling on my white shirt cuff as I try to balance everything—clipboard, resume and coffee—on the little writing part of the desk I am sitting at.

I have to compare what I am writing on the form to what I am writing on the resume so my lies match. When I bring back my disheveled clipboard, the glossy receptionists smile at a point beyond my head. They tell me to wait in a large cubicle where I sit nervously until a shrill woman in a bright yellow suit comes over and shakes my hand.

"Glad to meet ya," she says, in a thick New York accent.

Without waiting for a response, she asks, "So, how fast do ya type?" flicking ashes into a dark red ashtray. The red of the ashtray matches the red of her nails and the trim on the doors and windows. "Let's find out."

At first, I refuse to take a typing test. She views me suspiciously, as if I am saying something un-American.

"But I don't want a job typing." I try to tell her, "I'm trying to get away from all that. I want something—"

"Of course, you want something more, but we have to make sure of your skills."

When I ask her about the wonderful job I had responded to in the paper, the job in publishing, reading manuscripts, writing copy, she looks vague, as if she has never heard of that job. "Oh, that was taken."

I sit down to my typing test. My fingers feel thick and clumsy. I hear my father's words "How can you sit there and type all day!" and "You have to be realistic" as I type a page about a housewife who learns to consolidate tasks, do aerobics, learn a language, and word-process, all while her infant is having a nap. It's like some puzzle I can't figure out. I have to be realistic, yet not give up. But how can I stop typing all day unless I stop being realistic and start having a fantasy?

I do well on the typing test. After all, my life is typing.

Pat, my counselor, assures me she'll find me something in no time.

"Don't worry," she says, patting me like a dog, "I'll place you."

SINCE THAT'S EXACTLY what I'm afraid of, I decide to try Gregor's idea of unemployment. I go down to the unemployment office on one of those ugly New York days, when everyone seems to be talking too loudly and taking up one and a half seats on the subway. The office is crowded, there is only one line, and I read an entire science fiction book waiting for my number to be called, about aliens invading New York, and when I get to the front of the line, I'm so engrossed in the plot, I've almost forgotten why I'm there. I hand the man my form, where I have filled out "expected to perform menial duties not included in my job description" as my reason for wrongful termination. They tell me to call in for my telephone updates and give me a pamphlet on job hunting, and that, if all goes well and no one protests, I'll get my first check in three weeks.

AFTER MY EXERTION at the employment agency and unemployment agency, I stay in bed and read books on careers and eat Oreos.

How to Be What You Could Have Been. How to Find What You Were. I do exercises from the career books. What career did I want as a child? Thinking back is like falling down a long tunnel. I always believed I would be something wonderful when I grew up. Sometimes I imagined myself a dancer, wearing leotards with my hair piled high on my head; or I would be a veterinarian and cure lions and tigers at a circus. I gave up the idea of both early on. In dance class, there was a girl who

79

was so much better than me, Judy Hagan, that I decided not to compete, not to try so hard. The veterinarian idea died after I found a baby white rabbit in my backyard and I tried to nurse it back to life, unsuccessfully. My parents shook their heads and said it would have been kinder to leave it in the woods.

THE BOOKS TELL me to take small incremental steps to achieve my goal. I repeat that to myself. Small incremental steps. Do one thing you loved as a child. I decide to dip into my Christmas bonus and take a jazz dance class. Although I am much less flexible than everyone else, I can follow the routines, and get an approving nod from the instructor. It must be some left-over kinetic memory from my early dance classes, the ones that my mother sent me to. I loved those classes, swirling around with silky ribbons, being a tree, holding myself still longer than I believed possible. I stopped going when we started having recitals. At the thought of performing, my ribbons would fall to the floor limply and my tree would develop a terrible palsy.

Now, I feel the memory of those early classes in my joints, and in those memories of pliés and jettés is a kind of embedded hope, back before the first recital, when I thought everything was possible.

Chapter eight

GREGOR LEAVES A message on my machine: The last matinee of his play has been canceled, and he wants me to meet him for dinner.

We meet at a Spanish restaurant we used to go to when we were first dating. Why do people stop going out to restaurants when they start living in the same place? On the rare nights when he isn't rehearsing, we eat in pajamas in front of the television. It's cozy and comforting, but it lacks a certain glamour. I get ready slowly. Before I leave, I take a long hot bath and give myself a mineral mud facial. I shave my legs carefully, apply extra makeup, spray on perfume.

Gregor is late. I sip a glass of sangria and have an argument with myself. Half of me is incredibly understanding, making excuses for him, his audition class went late, he lost track of time, but the other half is small, hurt, incapable of understanding.

Gregor finally arrives and leans down to kiss me. I suppress the angry half unsuccessfully. "You know, I've been here for forty-five minutes!"

"I'm sorry, I couldn't help it, there was an accident at Fifty-ninth Street. Don't be mad."

"Okay, okay." I feel small and stupid now, as if I should have known about the accident. We only order appetizers, our favorite things on the menu, ceviche, manchego cheese, tiny sausages and potato frittatas. A woman sings Brazilian music in an alcove wearing a long tight dress that doesn't seem to allow her to breathe, much less sing.

WHEN WE GET home Gregor says he has something he wants to talk to me about.

"That sounds serious." My mind races: He's met someone else, he's gay, he's dying.

I grab his hand. "What is it?"

"Summer stock," says Gregor softly, stroking my hand. He has that look, that cautious look of an animal trainer circling a dangerous Bengal tiger, not knowing what to expect.

I look around the apartment, feeling trapped. "I move in and you want to go away."

"Liza, I just think it would be good stage experience. And you'll come down on the weekends."

"Where is it?"

"Well, I'm auditioning for Virginia. Someone got sick and a spot's opened up."

"Virginia's forever away. We used to go to camp there, in the Blue Ridge Mountains. When would you go?"

"Soon."

"When?"

"Next week."

I DON'T WANT Gregor to leave, but I make no effort to stop him. I encouraged him to start acting, and now I can't tell him not to go. I tell him I'll be fine. I have never loved him so much as at the moment he leaves.

"I'll call you," he tells me.

I nod.

"I'll write you."

I just stand there inside the apartment watching Gregor and his neatly packed suitcases on the other side of the door.

"Stop looking like the little matchgirl or I won't be able to go."

The elevator pings its arrival and Gregor kisses me and disappears.

*A*FTER HE IS gone, I regress. I eat foods that I liked as a child. Franco-American spaghetti from a can, Cheez Doodles, chocolate pudding. I feel like one of those characters in Bette's novels, comforted by a perfect soft-boiled egg. I eat in bed, surrounded by stuffed animals from *Wind in the Willows*, Toad and Mole and Rat. We bought them on a trip to Cape Cod. The apartment is a mess. I don't care. I'd like to blame Gregor's absence for my current state, but I've been feeling this way ever since I moved in. It was the same way when I moved in with Charles in San Francisco. Living with him, I was overtaken by inertia. It was all I could do to drag myself to my part-time job and home again to watch *All My Children* in the afternoon. For a while, I tried to start various businesses, greeting cards, catering, designing customized gift baskets, but I didn't have the strength to follow through. All I wanted to do was sleep.

The phone rings.

"What are you doing?" asks my sister sternly.

"Oh, I have a very exciting life. Right now, I am deciding between watching Ricki Lake and Oprah."

"You have to get out. It's a beautiful day and I'm going for a walk, you want to come?"

83

"I won't be much fun."

"That's fine."

WE WALK IN Central Park, shaded by trees, avoiding Rollerbladers and joggers. Why do people want to move so quickly? It is warm out but I wrap my sweater around me tighter. I feel frail and elderly.

We sit down on a bench.

"I don't know. There is nothing for me to do. Nothing I'm good at."

"That's not true."

I watch the dogs in the dog run.

"Did you know that when I was little I wanted to be a veterinarian?"

"No, I didn't."

"I did, but I never thought I could do it. You know, Gregor doesn't like dogs. If I even bring up getting a dog, he says he's allergic."

"Well you could still be a vet, go to school."

"I'd rather commit hari-kari than go back to school. You're the academic one."

"I saw an ad in the laundromat for a dog walker. It's off the books so you could still get unemployment."

"Well, it's an idea." I feel a warmth in my chest at the idea of dogs. "Remember Winnie?"

"Mom never liked her."

After we begged my father for years for a dog, my father brought home Winnie, a golden Collie puppy. We gave her to my mother for her birthday. Winnie was irresistible, except to my parents.

"They're not animal people," says my sister sadly.

"Sometimes I have dreams about her. Maybe I should call about that dog-walking job."

I ROUSE MYSELF TO see my therapist. I feel angry at her, at her silence.

When I do talk, for once I don't know what I'm going to say. Usually I rehearse my problems on the way over so I can sound spontaneous.

"You know, now that I'm not working, I'm not sure I'm going to be able to afford this anymore." As I say the words, I know that I have set off a small bomb. This is the one thing therapists can't deal with. You could tell them you've had sex with a close relative or dreamed of killing them and they will nod sympathetically. But if you tell them you might cut the forty-five-minute umbilical cord, they lose all objectivity.

We argue for the rest of the session over this. She threatens me with loss of psychological benefits, that I won't be able to stop my patterns, that I will keep repeating myself in a never-ending loop of neurosis. That I need her. I tell her that she is not my first priority. It gives me a weird satisfaction to see her lose her calm objectivity.

"Will I see you next week?" she asks me at the end of the session.

"I'll have to see how it goes. With money. I'll call you."

On the way home, I decide to call about the dog-walking job.

G REGOR CALLS AS I am heating up some Chef Boyardee ravioli. I feel awkward.

"How are you?" he asks.

"Fine. I miss you." I feel this comes out as a reproach and I don't wait for his *I miss you too*. "Are you busy?"

"Yeah, the schedule's a killer. We rehearse all morning for the play we're doing next week, and we have run-throughs in the afternoon for the play that's on. I'm in *Major Barbara*, *Crossing Delancey* and *On the Road*."

"They're doing Kerouac?"

"Well it's an upbeat musical, sort of like *Hair*, if you can believe it. Are you okay?"

"Sure, I guess, how are the people, the other actrons?"

"They're okay. Young. I've got a song, can you believe it? In Kerouac."

"Cool."

"Listen, they're calling me, I've got to run, I love you."

"Me, too. Don't fall in love with any ingenues."

"You know, it's funny, Liza, there aren't any girls down here, not even one, we have to do everything in drag."

"Ha ha. Hey, you're not doing any kissing scenes, are you?"

"Just one."

"Great," I say. A vision of Gregor entwined with a young blond actress pops into my head. I push it out, stirring the ravioli harder with my wooden spoon. "You know what, I got a job!"

"That's great. I'm sorry but I've really got to run. I'll call you in a couple of days."

"Okay." When I get off the phone and start eating my crushed ravioli, I realize he never asked what my job was.

I'M CONVINCED GREGOR is never coming back. He is either going to run off with some summer stock ingenue or die in a tragic accident, a large lighting fixture falling on his head, a sword fight gone wrong.

"I don't know what you're worrying about," says my friend Elinor. "You should see the way he looks at you."

"That's the point, he's not here looking at me, and he might see someone else while he is not here looking at me."

WHEN I GO to get my mail in the morning, I find a computer disk from my father for an astrology program. It seems such a weird thing for him to send me, but he probably figures I'd be into anything weird. He encloses a handwritten note with it. This makes me smile. I remember being at camp and getting typewritten letters from my father analyzing my attitude toward my counselor. I put the disk in my computer and figure out how to print out my chart. It is full of tiny symbols and degrees and I have no idea what it means.

I GO TO Barnes & Noble and buy books on astrology, colorful books that hold promises of clearing up uncertainties and predicting the future. I look up my chart and then my sister's. We are both heavily influenced by Pluto, a strong controlling figure, probably my father. It's true, when I was little I thought my father was the supreme being, that he knew everything, had done everything.

The entire day passes in a flash as I nibble ginger cookies and pore over the astrology books.

MY NEW JOB is walking a dog for two old ladies. Their dog is named Obey but she hardly ever does. It forces me to get exercise, as they are afraid of Obey's getting osteoporosis and make me promise to walk her two miles every day. Can dogs even get osteoporosis? Obey is a girl and I can imagine them debating on whether to give her estrogen replacement therapy.

I TELL EVERYONE I know about my new interest in the occult, but no one I know is especially encouraging about my pursuit of astrology; in fact, they look at me as if I have gone off the deep end.

Even my sister looks skeptical.

"Well, I just want to see where it leads, it's fun. You know, people actually pay for this stuff."

"I suppose. I still think you should go back to school, maybe in psychology."

"They have an astrology school in England, it's very well respected."

When I tell Gwendolyn and Amelia, the old ladies, they are thrilled and they ruffle through yellowing papers looking for their birth times.

I TAKE ANOTHER part-time job at the tiny Coffee Clatch near my house at a shockingly low salary, but they say they won't declare me to the IRS. With the dog walking and Gregor's sending half the rent, I can just about make it. I still haven't heard from the unemployment people yet. I can't believe how long it takes. At the café, I eat unpopular sandwiches and pieces of pound cake that are not symmetrical. At night, I eat soup or canned spaghetti, sometimes a vegetable. I take dance classes twice a week and work on my turnout, which is abominable. At home, I work on aspects, constructing charts of everyone I know, trying to see patterns.

"You're turning into a hermit," says Elinor. "Just because Gregor's gone doesn't mean you have to go into mourning."

"Elly, do you know that you have a grand cross in your chart, which is a very rare aspect?"

"Really, tell me more."

I DON'T FEEL like a hermit. I just don't feel like going out. Ever since I moved in with Gregor, I have focused on him, when is he coming home, when are we going to have sex, are we happy, is it working out? But now that he's gone, I am forced to turn inward and focus on me.

I DON'T GO back to my therapist. She leaves messages on my machine, telling me to reconsider.

D O YOU EVER think of letting your hair grow up?" says Gwendolyn as I bring Obey home, the both of us exhausted from a long walk around the park.
"You mean grow out, not grow up," says Amelia.
I sink into a chintzy chair. "Grow out? No not really."
"Oh leave the girl alone," says Amelia. "I was just saying, it is a little severe."
"Well, maybe you're right, maybe I should grow it out."
"Here, have some more tea."
I smell the sassafras tea they always serve me. It smells like newly mown grass. I enjoy the smell of it more than the flavor.

WHEN I GET home I turn on the TV. I watch too much TV. It keeps me company. I watch a TV show about a medical center and there is a policeman who gets hurt in an elevator accident, badly. He's not going to make it. He is gay. The guy's partner who sent him into the elevator is crying.
"I'm sorry," he keeps repeating, "I'm sorry," and the guy who is dying keeps saying, "I'm scared, I'm scared of dying."
I start to cry.

Tad calls me. Since the vacuuming incident, he's been calling me every few weeks to check up on me. He won't criticize Darla directly, but he seems worried about me. I turn off the show, gladly, blowing my nose. I tell him about the episode.

"Are you watching it?" I ask him.

"No, I had to turn it off, it was too depressing. Do you ever notice that the gay guys are always the ones who die on television? So how are you? Listen, do you want to go to a Fourth of July party?"

"What, did you run out of straight women?"

"Something like that."

"Well, if I can fit it into my busy schedule."

I CALL MY sister.

"You have to come with me. It'll be fun."

"I don't think so. Anyway, I thought you were mad at Tad."

"He's all right, under that bitchy exterior. He even offered to lend me money."

"Did you take it?"

"No, but it was sweet. Anyway, don't change the subject. I want you to come."

"Is anybody else from the office going to be there?"

"No. Can you believe this? He thinks they don't know he's gay. Look, I think it'll be fun."

"If it's like that other party . . ."

"No, Tad has normal friends. Trust me."

Chapter

nine

I GET DRESSED up for the party. I haven't done this in a long time. Since Gregor's been away at summer stock, I've been wearing my most comfortable, worn-in T-shirts and my old baggy shorts. Now, I pull out an old Betsy Johnson dress from the dark Siberia of my closet, a dress I haven't fit into for three and a half years. The dress is short and tight with a leopard print. Last time I wore it was at a party with Charles in San Francisco, and I remember him commenting on how revealing it was, liking it and disapproving of it at the same time. Although I miss Gregor, it's kind of refreshing getting dressed without a male opinion, putting on exactly what I want at this exact moment. I put on my favorite martini earrings, one earring is the glass, the other the shaker. I mousse up my short hair and look in the mirror, seeing someone unfamiliar, someone attractive. You'd think one's own face would be familiar after all these years, but the more I look at it, the more strange it becomes. Who is this person? I know the facts: I normally have short brown hair, hazel eyes, an oval face. Lately,

I've been dyeing my hair Auburn Sunset. I have been called pretty, or at least attractive by people, sometimes beautiful by people who love me. But how many times have I looked at myself and seen flaws, tiny lines, irregularities, a general look of uncertainty? But tonight I look and I am pleased. My hair looks right and my mascara goes on without major incident. Someone could look at me in this leopard outfit and think, Here's a girl who lives an exciting life, someone who has a life, not someone who lies in bed eating Oreos. I have actually lost weight, although it's probably from the long dog walks in Central Park and my dance classes, not the Oreo eating. My body approximates the slim body I remember from high school. It makes me want to hear the music from my teenage years, so I put on an old disco CD I bought from a record club and dance around the apartment, my high heels slipping on the wood floor.

I TAKE A CAB over to Tad's, clutching my little round silver purse like a talisman.

I have always been good at parties. Every year since I can remember, my mother had a party for her dream students, a party that ended in all the students dancing in a large circle, dancing and hugging and telling their dreams to each other until late in the night.

My father and my sister would stand off to the side, leaning on the kitchen door, voluntary outsiders. My father was patronizing and indulgent toward my mother and her students. "All that touchy-feely stuff," he would say, as if speaking of a backward country. Handsome and aloof, he would stand off to the side with my sister, analyzing and critiquing, the two of them part of a special secret society. I would flit from the dream group, who laughed and danced with me, to the grown-up talk of my father and sister.

"YOU'RE THE SOCIAL one," my mother always told me, and I would act social, talking to strangers, whether or not I felt like it.

According to family legend, and repeated too often for my liking at dinner parties, I have always had a knack for going up to a complete stranger and asking them a telling personal question. There was the time I went up to a newly divorced friend of my mother's and asked in my loud, six-year-old way, "Are you married?" and the woman burst into tears. My parents thought this was hilarious.

*T*HE CAB DROPS me off in front of a large anonymous apartment building and I glide up in the elevator to the eighteenth floor. I've been to Tad's apartment before, for an office party, and as the doors open, it surprises me again with its beauty. It's his life's work, his pièce de résistance, every marbled wall, every sconce, every shade of ivory lovingly picked out by him. Like me, he loves antiques and Pre-Raphaelite paintings. Before anyone notices I've arrived, I wander around, admiring the absence of Fourth of July decorations. I see there is a long table laid out with exotic foods and a bar set up in the kitchen. I wonder if Bette is here yet? She promised she'd make an extra effort to be social tonight.

AT THE PARTY, I drink too much wine and break a glass. I don't mean to, but I am gesturing too expansively.

"Oh no," I say to Tad's boyfriend Ron, trying to hide the shattered pieces. I am mortified.

"Don't worry," he says, sweeping it up deftly, "I never liked those glasses anyway."

"Don't tell Tad. Please, promise me."

He looks alarmed by my distress, as if he is afraid I might break something else.

"It's okay, I won't tell him, I like having little secrets from him anyway." Whenever I break things, which is not infrequent, I feel terrible. I feel like I have failed some important test, that I will never get anything right, that I am clumsy and stupid. When Gregor breaks things, it's the thing's fault, for being slippery, or dangerous, or in the wrong place. I always blame myself, not the thing. I have noticed that people who succeed in life have an ability to only take credit for things, and not accept any responsibility for things going wrong. I, on the other hand, absorb blame like a sponge.

I move away from the scene of the crime and eat skewered portobello mushrooms and some kind of smoked meat over by the buffet.

TAD'S PARTY IS successful, as are all his parties. He is very comfortable in the host mode, making sure everyone has drinks, introducing people, creating a space where people can feel brave and talk to people they wouldn't dream of otherwise. I am the only one he's invited from the office and I feel special. I can't even believe I worked there now. Sometimes, I'll wake up and have a moment of Monday morning dread, but then I remember, no, I may be broke and careerless, but at least I don't have to put on panty hose and go into that dysfunctional office.

I GREET SOME people. They look vaguely back at me, not sure where they know me from. I don't volunteer anything. I have decided if anyone asks me what I do, I will say that I'm occupationally challenged. I look around for my sister.

"Excuse me," I hear someone saying, right next to me, and look up at a man with dark eyes that a romance novel would describe as piercing.

"Hi," I say stupidly, staring up at him. I immediately feel guilty.

The man reaches across me for a skewer of shrimp and carefully dips it into a mysterious sauce.

He appears content as he eats it, like a great big dark cat.

He finishes the shrimp and starts on some pâté. It feels intimate, watching him eating. He hands me a cracker with pate on it.

"Try this, it's delicious."

"Thanks."

"It's a great apartment, isn't it?" he says, looking at me too intensely for my comfort.

"Yes, it is." I fiddle with the stem of my wineglass. This is exactly how I broke the other one.

"So, where do you live?" he asks, leaning in a little, as if he expects to be invited there very soon.

It seems like we have missed some important conversational steps here. I feel the thin fabric of my dress moving against my skin, the cold glass in my hand, the warm press of all the people around us. Where is my sister, anyway? This is the kind of man I used to be attracted to, dangerously attracted to, the kind of man who is never really there when you need him. I see the whole progress of our affair in the pause before I answer him, the steamy sex, the way his hands would move over me, slowly and deliberately. He'd be sincere during, but afterward, he'd evaporate. I'll call you, he'd say, walking out the door, and he would, but it would be a little too late and he'd be a little too distant.

"I live with my boyfriend, uptown," I say, struggling to picture Gregor.

He smiles, taking a small step backward and I feel a secret glow of gratitude to Gregor, for saving me from this man.

"I'm going to get a drink." Now I'm eager to leave him, as if I am the one who has callously taken what I wanted.

I RUN INTO Tad near the wine bottles.

"Having fun?" says Tad, filling up my glass with Bordeaux.

"Yeah, absolutely fabulous party." We kiss the air near each other's faces. "Hey Tad, do they ask about me, you know, at work?"

"Yes, Darla always says you are a sweet girl and hopes you'll be better soon."

"Do you think that was too much, that story about me having a nervous breakdown?"

"No, it worked like a charm. Otherwise, she would have hated you. Aren't you glad I didn't invite her?"

"Affirmative. I'm so glad I don't work there anymore. It's like I can breathe now. Have you seen my sister?"

"She's over there. She's fine. A real party animal."

"Right. Where is she? I don't see her."

"Trust me, she's fine."

"I just want to see for myself."

I look around and find my sister talking animatedly to a man by the refrigerator. I can tell she is interested in him by the way she keeps playing with her hair, which I convinced her to wear down.

"Tad, don't tell me he's one of the boys."

"Let me put on my gaydar." Tad puts his hands up to his eyes like he is putting on special binoculars. He looks intently at the man for a moment and shakes his head.

"No, he's not gay, he's my brother."

"Isn't that, 'He ain't heavy, he's my brother'?"

"No, he's really my brother—Lawrence. The good one. The successful one. The tall one."

"You're kidding, right?"

"Do you want me to introduce you?"

"No, wait, maybe they're in the middle of something."

"What, talking?"

"No, some subtle exchange of pheromones that they're not even aware of. If this works out, Tad, you know what this would make us, don't you? Related."

Tad pretends to look horrified. "We're trying to marry up in my family, not down."

"Bitch. Just because they're talking at a party, it doesn't mean your family bloodline is going to be tainted."

"That's how it begins," he says dramatically. "Talking at a party."

"Change of subject. Who was that guy I was talking to, you know the one with the dark hair, the tall one."

"Yes, I saw you. That's Anthony. Cute, huh?"

"Yes."

"He's very mysterious, we don't even have a phone number for him, just a beeper. Ron thinks he's into organized crime, or a spy. He's divorced, in case you're interested."

"I'm not."

"Well, that's not what it looked like."

"Okay, I confess. I am, but I shouldn't be."

"You wouldn't!" Now Tad looks genuinely horrified.

I always wrongly assume that because Tad's gay, he leads a wild life, but I don't think he's ever slept with anyone he hasn't been seriously involved with, and he has probably never had a one-night stand, or woken up some place not remembering how he got there.

I smile. "No, I wouldn't, but I certainly was tempted. Aren't you ever?"

"Sure, but it's too messy."

At this moment, Tad's boyfriend comes over and puts his arms around both of us. We must look guilty because he says, "Okay, what are you two up to?"

"We were having a deep philosophical discussion," I say. "You know, Sartre, Camus, the meaning of life."

Ron smiles. He's a little older, more tanned than Tad. He looks like he's had more of a past. He grins and looks like he doesn't believe me. "You know what this party needs? Dancing!!"

"Yes, disco, put this on—I was listening to it at home." I pull out my disco CD from my silver purse. He puts it on and "We Are Family" booms through the apartment. I grab Ron and start to dance. I swirl around feeling lighter, freer. It's as if I had buried this whole part of me, the me that swirled around with the colorful dreamers, the part that men find attractive, that now does the bump with Ron. The music seems to infect everyone with the same feeling and other people start to dance, putting down their drinks on ledges, tables, looking around for partners. I look around for the mysterious Anthony but instead I see my sister dancing with Tad's brother, and for a moment, everything is perfect. Someone calls out that the fireworks are happening and we all rush out to the tiny terrace, crowding around, looking at the luminous circles of expanding light, as if a distant giant were blowing smoke rings in our direction. Everyone watches the fireworks, mesmerized, one after the other, until they dissolve into the blackness. I wonder why fireworks always have to be round. Someone next to me says "Happy Fourth of July" to me, and I clink my glass with his. I turn around and am staring straight at the guy I was talking to, the spy, the organized-crime kingpin, the mysterious Anthony.

He smiles at me, "Happy Independence Day."

"Ditto."

"Still living with that guy?"

"Yes."

"Tad tells me he's an actor."

I smile, surprised and flattered. "You asked Tad about him?"

"Is he good?"

I nod and as everyone spills back into the apartment after the fireworks, I have to physically force myself to move away from Anthony, as if he is the center of a magnetic force field.

I AM FINALLY STANDING next to my sister, who is eating random foods by the buffet.

I am shocked by her culinary choices. "I thought you hated sun-dried tomatoes."

"What made you think that?" my sister asks dreamily, a toothpick skewered in a food she normally never would eat, food she calls "yuppie food," food she hates. She is eating as if all the food is the same, random and meaningless.

"Are you okay?"

"Of course I am."

"So," I ask, "what did you think?"

"About what?"

"You know, about Tad's brother, what's his name?"

"Lawrence, he's very nice. He's an architect. We were talking about Gaudi."

"Is Gaudy that guy who did those weird, curvy buildings in Spain?"

"It's Gaudi, spelled G-A-U-D-I, pronounced Gowdy not Gaudy. It's funny, we've both always wanted to go to Barcelona."

"And . . . ?"

"He asked for my number," my sister says, blushing.

"Great, that's great."

My sister nods and eats a piece of sushi as if she is a million miles away.

"So, what's he like?"

"He likes Jane Austen, and he hates Rollerblades."

"Sounds perfect. What should I wear to the wedding?"

"Don't say that. Don't jinx it."

WHEN I GET home there is a message from Gregor on my answering machine. We have separate phones, his idea, not mine. He said he needed a separate line for his acting career, that he couldn't afford to miss a call. It blinks at me reproachfully. I press the play button.

"Hi, how are you?"

I talk back to the machine.

"Fine."

"I was thinking about you."

"Sure you were." I feel guilty, as if he knows I was considering, if only for a moment, sleeping with someone else.

Gregor wants me to come down and visit him, maybe for the last weekend of the run, and then we could come back home together.

I have no number to call him in Virginia. I don't even think they have working phones in the rooms, just a pay phone in the hall. I sit down at his desk and leaf through old bills and scraps of paper, receipts, pencils, his old acting diary. Gregor has forbidden me to touch anything on his desk. Why does he keep all this junk anyway? I spin around on the creaky wheels of his old wooden desk chair, around and around, searching for traces of him.

Chapter ten

"I NEED SOME UNDERWEAR," my sister says purposefully, heading off to the lingerie department. We are at a discount department store in the financial district. I follow behind, my eye caught by bright lilacs and greens, colors I would never wear.

Since the party last week, my sister and Lawrence have talked on the phone every day and seen each other four times, once for dinner at his house. He made risotto with porcino mushrooms and they talked for hours. "It's amazing how much we have in common," she told me. They haven't had sex yet but in one week, her entire personality has changed. A week ago, she was solitary, introspective and shy. Now she is vivacious and bubbly.

I examine the underwire on a bra, twisting it one way and then the other. Why do I have such trouble finding something attractive *and* functional?

"Bette, do you ever notice how the underwire in all your bras falls apart at the same time? Bette where are you? Am I talking to myself here?"

"No. I'm listening."

I walk around the rack to the sound of her voice. My sister is perusing red lacy bikinis. I've seen her underwear, dozens of pairs of white cotton panties with little flowers on them. She looks at me like I've caught her doing something shameful.

"Liza, don't look at me like that."

I smile. "I didn't say a word. But I thought you guys were going to wait a bit."

"Well, I want to be prepared."

"Here," I say, pulling out the matching bra in her size. "Might as well go for the whole seductress outfit. You wouldn't want to be uncoordinated for your first time, would you?"

Bette buys the underwear, a black dress, and a pair of heels. I don't buy anything. Nothing is right.

IT'S HOT AND sunny and we eat lunch sitting outside at a Mexican restaurant under an umbrella. We order quesadillas and margaritas. Bette looks distracted. Since the party, she always looks distracted. I am tempted to stop and ask her, "What have you done with my sister?"

I lick the salt off my glass. "I brought your charts."

My sister leans forward eagerly. "So what do they say, about us?"

"Let's see. Well, your moon is rising in Lawrence's seventh house, and that's one of the best aspects you can have for a serious relationship."

"Really." My sister sounds so happy it seems dangerous.

I feel compelled to tell her to be cautious, that everything is not what it seems. "Well there are some negatives, too."

My sister the professor holds her arms stiffly in front of her and swivels from side to side, imitating a robot: "Danger, danger Will Robinson."

"Do you want to hear this or not?" I say sternly.

"Yes, I'll be good."

"Well he has some heavy Pluto influences. He could be quite possessive, and jealous."

My sister tries to look serious but I can tell she doesn't see this as a problem. At this moment I could tell her he was Jack the Ripper and she wouldn't think it was a problem.

I look at the chart more carefully, seeing something I missed. "Oh my God!"

"What is it. Is it bad?"

"It's this double Scorpio thing. He's a sex maniac!" I blurt out.

"You're kidding." She sounds more intrigued than alarmed. "So when do you want to meet him? You didn't even get to talk to him at the party."

"I don't know. I don't think I'm ready yet."

"You would like him. He's different from Tad. Calmer."

"Tad's all right."

"Well, let me know." She is silent for a moment and then says, "By the way, have you heard from Gregor?"

"Yeah, he wants me to go down to summer stock next week. It's the last week, and he wants to rent a car so we can drive back together."

"So, what's the matter?"

"I don't know. I guess I'm afraid that things will be different now."

"Liza, don't be silly, he's only been gone six weeks."

"Six weeks is a long time. Look what happened to you in a week. And speaking of sex, before he left we weren't exactly having a lot of it."

"Couples go through phases. It doesn't mean anything. Are you going to eat this?" Bette points to the last wedge of quesadilla.

"Go ahead. I guess everything seems so unsettled."

Chapter eleven

MY TRAIN IS running late. Since Gregor has been away at summer stock, I've developed this habit of talking to myself. "Everything's fine," I tell myself now, as if talking to a small child. "You can buy that nice fruit-and-cheese plate in the dining car. He will still love you when you get there." I repeat something my friend Elinor says to me: "Life is a process, not an event." It settles me down although I'm not quite sure what it means.

GREGOR MEETS ME at the station. He borrowed the company truck. He is glad to see me, but he seems sad to be leaving summer stock. I try not to take it personally.

"It's the work," he tells me. "Doing plays every day, not having to go to a job, to be able to support myself doing this."

"I understand." I start to feel small, abandoned, imagining

more summer stock, plays, Gregor on location for months and months.

"I wish I could do that and be near you."

When I hear the words "near you" my jealousy and bad feelings melt away for a moment.

"You will, you're very good."

"Well, tell me that later, after you see the play."

"Did I tell you my sister met someone?"

"Oh, yeah? Who?"

"Tad's brother Lawrence. You know, Tad from my old job, at a party."

I think about the party. About that cute guy I met. Anthony. Keeping a secret from Gregor feels strange to me.

"What's Lawrence like?"

"According to my sister, he's a saint. He cooks. He cleans. He likes to go shopping for shoes. According to his chart, he's a sex maniac."

Gregor glances over at me but does not respond to this. "What does he do?"

"He's an architect. He just designed a pool out in the Hamptons."

DURING THE DAY, Gregor has rehearsal for a benefit performance they're doing. I walk around the campus. I feel slightly disoriented, the way I felt in college most of the time. I wander around a little lake and feel a necessity to come to a decision about something. I have my book of career exercises with me. My next exercise is to pick my ideal family from a pool of anyone, dead or alive, people who would totally support me. I pick the Dalai Lama as an uncle because he always seems cheerful and wise. Barbara Pym as an aunt. I'm stuck on parents. It seems disloyal to choose other ones. I ponder Mr. Rogers for a father and Virginia Woolf for a mother. I move on to the next exercise: Imagine the perfect day. But before I get to it, sleep overtakes me. I lie down on the long green grass, hoping there aren't any little bugs in it.

THE THEATER IS crowded. I take a small metal seat in the aisle. Gregor's scene is toward the end. My mind wanders through the monologues. Why do they always have so many monologues? You're absorbed in a play, and all of a sudden, there is an actor yelling at you. It's exhausting.

Gregor's scene is on. It's from a Harold Pinter play. He is talking to a woman, torturing her.

"Have they been raping you?" he asks her in an evil slinky voice.

Louder: "How many times?"

And meaner:

"How many times!"

The woman is crying, sobbing on stage, hysterical. I want to hit him, yell at him to stop.

I saw him run through his lines this afternoon but he did it differently, not as if he meant it. Now, he is scaring me.

AFTER THE SHOW, they have a little party, with bowls of potato chips, pretzels and dried-up-looking pizzas. Gregor introduces me to everyone, and several people take me aside to tell me how lucky I am, how wonderful Gregor is. A tiny woman in a long flowery dress comes up to me. I realize she was the one being tortured.

"Oh, you are Gregor's girlfriend. You know, between scenes, he keeps me laughing and laughing." She smiles and touches my arm and I try to smile back with equal force.

"Great," I say.

"Gregor's a riot," says another actor I've been introduced to but have forgotten his name. "He's so funny."

I love Gregor but I never thought of him as being especially comedic. It's as if he has this whole secret life I didn't know about where he is the life of the party. I feel extraneous and I can't think of a thing to say to anyone. They all have big personalities, and I feel as if I've misplaced mine.

Gregor keeps coming up to me and touching me on the arm, trying to keep me included, but I feel totally out of things.

"Are you okay?"

I am supposed to be good at parties, good with strangers, but I have never felt worse at it.

"Fine."

THE ACTORS GIVE each other postcards, with sayings on the back. Everyone is hugging and kissing. It's like the last day of high school, with everyone leaving tearful messages and saying all these things they don't mean to people they'll probably never see again.

Sinking into a couch on the outskirts of things, I watch as one of the actors lies on the floor, moaning softly, a wet washcloth pressed to his forehead. Two of the very young actresses lie next to him, urging him to eat a Snickers.

"Come on, sweetie, it's good for you."

"You need your strength."

When Gregor comes over I ask, "What's wrong with him?"

"He missed his entrance, and now he's saying it's because his blood sugar dipped dangerously low."

Gregor rolls his eyes to show me what he thinks of this. "Talk about your drama queen."

AFTER THE PLAY, we go back to Gregor's room. He is exuberant.

"So you liked it?"

"You were great. Very believable."

Gregor's room is like any tiny single room in any college dorm. The old metal desk, the anemic-looking bed, a lamp over the desk and one over the bed providing inadequate lighting.

"So, here we are," Gregor says, showing me the room with a sweep of his hand. He still looks like the character in the scene to me, taller, larger than himself. Even his gestures seem bigger. "What's the matter?"

"I don't know. I feel like I don't know you anymore."

"Come on."

"These people see this whole other side of you. They keep telling me how funny you are."

"Is that so terrible?" Gregor is smiling now, and I can tell these people don't say any of this mushy stuff to him. "What else do they say?"

"Oh, how great you are, you know, mostly how funny."

"So, don't you think I'm funny?"

"No, yes, you're funny, it's . . ."

"Forget about what they think. Believe me, they're more fun when they're up on stage saying someone else's lines. Off-stage, they want to be told how great they are. Anyway, we're here now, alone. So, what should we do?" Gregor puts on an innocent expression and slides his hand up under my dress.

"I don't know." His fingers reach up higher, inside my underwear. I try to make my breath steady.

"Did you miss me?" he asks softly.

"Yes."

We roll over onto the bed, and start touching each other. I run my hands under his shirt and remember how much I miss touching him. He is the first man I ever really felt comfortable touching. For a long time, I wouldn't touch men, especially their penises. I'd been traumatized once by a guy saying I'd been too rough, so I stopped altogether. I had sex with men for years never touching that significant part. But with Gregor, I always loved touching him all over. "This is your spine," I'd say, running my fingers over each bony vertebra. "These are your legs," I would whisper, running my hands up the muscles on the back of his thighs. "This is your penis," I'd say triumphantly, running my fingers over its silky length.

But here, in Virginia, on this little bed, Gregor is familiar yet unfamiliar. He starts undressing me, sweeping me into sex before I have time to get excited enough. He has the intensity I always want, but for some reason it's distancing me from him. I have a feeling I used to have in high school, necking with some guy who was programmed for one objective, going as far as possible, as fast as possible, before you change your mind. Now, like then, my excitement is turning into a self-protective numbness. Gregor is kissing my neck, my breasts, touching me everywhere. He takes off the rest of my clothes and he is grabbing me hard, pressing me against him. He puts a condom on and I want to protest, "Not yet," but I can't. It's as if we are onstage. He is rougher than usual, as though he wants to imprint himself in me.

Afterward, Gregor strokes my stomach.

"You've lost weight," he says.

I don't say anything so he doesn't see how I feel, but I curl up next to him. Now he feels more like himself, as he strokes my hair, softly, hypnotically, until I start to feel desire climbing through me.

"That felt different, didn't it," Gregor says.

"Yes."

"You didn't . . . I mean, it was more for me, wasn't it?"

I nestle my head deeper in his shoulder. "I have to get used to you again."

He kisses me on the mouth. "Well, we have plenty of time for that."

Chapter twelve

W E HAVE TO make plans for Mom's sixty-fifth birthday. You know, it's this Sunday!"

"I'm not sure I can go," Bette says, and I feel a wave of irritation sweep through me. I know the reason she can't go is Lawrence but I ask her anyway.

"We're going to be in the Hamptons. It's business."

"But it's Mommy's birthday, you have to come!"

My sister sounds exasperated, like I can't understand a simple concept. "Liza, I said I'll try, but I don't know if I can make it."

MY SISTER'S RECKLESSNESS fills me with terror. She is so willing to give up her normal life, her old life, for the promise of a new life with Lawrence. Each time she says how great it is going, I get a shiver of fear. Why do I believe anything good has to end in disaster? I long to find Lawrence's dark side, so that I can protect my sister from disappointment.

It's ironic. I worried so much about my sister not meeting anyone. For years, I encouraged her to put herself out there, came up with little schemes, even goaded her into going to the matchmaker; but now that Bette's actually found someone, I'm worried.

The only constant here is my worrying. It's as if I believe that only a properly applied concentration of my worrying can hold things together.

LAWRENCE LIVES IN Westchester. Bette packs bags and unpacks bags with abandon, leaving toothbrushes and small personal effects at his house. Bette, who has stayed in the cool oasis of her apartment for more Friday nights than I can remember, claiming that she preferred to have time alone, that she needed it after the long week of academic infighting, now uses her home like a flight attendant.

WE NO LONGER meet for our weekend brunches at the Mansion.

"We've been cooking breakfast," she tells me proudly. "Omelets."

"I thought you couldn't abide more than a piece of toast and a scrape of butter in the mornings."

"I know, it's funny, but I've grown quite fond of Lawrence's western omelets. He's a great cook. You'll have to come over sometime and we'll make you one."

I hang up the phone, muttering, "western omelets."

"What's for breakfast?" Gregor calls out as I walk into the bedroom, where he is still cocooned in the covers like a giant baby.

"Lawrence is making western omelets in Westchester. They've been seeing each other two weeks, and now she'll eat anything."

"It sounds like you're jealous."

I throw my favorite hairbrush at him. It misses him, hitting the wall instead. When it snaps in half, I start to cry.

114

Once I start crying, I can't stop. I'm not sure what I'm crying for, but there is a sharp pain inside my chest, and the tears seem to be trying to release it.

I sit stiffly on the edge of the bed. Gregor pulls me gently down toward him. He puts his hands on my shoulders.

"I can't believe you think I'm like that."

"Liza, I'm sorry, I was just kidding, you're not jealous. It's something else." He gets up and looks under the bed for my hairbrush. It's a plastic travel hairbrush that folds in half. I would have thrown it in the garbage, but Gregor finds the pieces and patiently fits them together until they join with a satisfying snap. I feel calmer watching him.

I don't want to talk about my sister, but I can't help myself. "You know, he wants her there all the time. She'll probably move out there in a few days."

Gregor looks appalled. "He's giving men a bad name." He unfolds my brush and starts slowly brushing my hair. My father used to brush my hair when I was little. I had long hair and I hated washing it, but I loved having my father's attention as he tried to comb through the knots without hurting me.

NOW, A RUSH of warmth for Gregor sweeps over me, and the pressure inside my chest suddenly lifts and vanishes. I sit behind him and kiss his neck. "Thanks for fixing my brush," I say, kissing softly all down his neck to his spine. He sits quietly but I can tell he likes it.

I slide my hands under his T-shirt and he says, "What are you doing?" as if he has no idea that in a few moments we will be making love, but I see him glancing over to the night table to make sure we haven't run out of condoms.

LYING HERE, WITH Gregor softly sleeping, I am more relaxed, almost happy. But why do I get so upset about my sister, why do

I feel so responsible? She's the oldest, she should be the one worrying.

I have always felt responsible. When I was little, my parents were very busy. They were successful and far away, and together, like a small constellation just out of my reach. Consequently, I was a fearful yet reckless child. During the day, I loved to stand atop the thin railing of our outdoor porch, pretending to fall, but at night I would be paralyzed by the darkness, the noises, the gargoyles on the banister outside my room. Lying in my single bed with my teddy bear, I would be soaked in sweat and fear. If I moved one inch, *they* would get me.

My parents taught me to figure things out on my own, and I got the idea that if I did everything very carefully, if I kept up a watchful vigilance on all the dangerous shapes in the dark, the things that could go wrong, I could control them.

Whenever my parents were out very late at night, at conferences, or parties, I imagined them dying in a car crash. It was only at the moment I heard them pulling into the driveway that I would relax my tense muscles, believing my vigilance alone had saved them from certain death.

ELINOR CALLS ME from Boston and I go into the kitchen with the portable phone and tell her about my sister and what's been going on.

"She's practically living in Westchester. I don't even know if she goes into her office anymore."

"I would do the same thing," Elinor tells me, "if I met someone. I'd want to be with him all the time. You have to remember, she's been alone for a long time."

"You would?"

"Yes, I would. Listen, maybe you're just feeling a little left out. Now she's the one with the relationship that takes up her time, not you."

"You're probably right. You're going to have to move back and take over as my big sister."

"I love you, but I'm not moving back to New York."

I GET OFF the phone and take Gregor some Raisin Bran in bed.

"You're the best," he says happily.

"Just remember that."

I VOW TO be nicer to my sister, I vow not to say anything negative about Lawrence, no matter how wonderful he is. Maybe Elinor is right, maybe I do feel left out. I remember a summer when I was seven and my sister was twelve. She and her best friend Helen, after closeting themselves in the attic one day, came down and started talking to tiny perfectly formed people they gently took out of their ears and placed on their palms. I could almost see the little people but not quite. They were just out of the range of my vision.

"You'll see them when you're older," they told me confidentially. "You'll have your own people." I knew I'd never have my own people. My sister and Helen were special, older. They would always be privy to a whole secret world at which I could only peer through the window.

Chapter thirteen

N SUNDAY, WE take the bus up to my parents' house in Woodstock.

"You're sure you don't mind?" I ask Gregor, as the bus stops.

"No, it's fine."

It's amazing to me how much Gregor doesn't mind my parents. I don't know why I'm so shocked. As far back as I can remember, my friends always loved my parents, wanted to trade with me, told me my parents were cool. My friends could talk to my parents about controversial issues, tell them their personal problems, no one would care if you said a curse word. Most of all, they loved my parents because they usually weren't there. After school, the house was empty and we could do what we wanted. Even when they were there, I could come and go as I pleased. I didn't even have to sneak into the house at three in the morning like my friend Elinor, because my parents trusted me. They slept soundly under their blue comforter no matter what time I came home.

Gregor and I are only staying one night. My parents are

waiting for us. I can sense them from miles away. I see them from the driveway as we pull up in our taxi. They stand on the porch, waiting.

Both my parents seem older, frailer to me, ever since I saw my mother in the hospital for her blood pressure incident. Whenever I ask her about her health, she says she's fine. Both of my parents are still active, still teaching, but it's as if they were forty-five for twenty years and now all of a sudden they're sixty-five, and I can't prevent what is happening to them. I look at my parents carefully and try to gauge if they're really OK. I feel a sudden pang of guilt, as though if anything does happen to them, it will be my fault.

I LOOK AROUND for my brother. He is staying up with my parents for a few weeks.

Once I get inside the house, with its familiar quilts and pottery and African sculpture, I find him on the couch. I sit next to him and we punch each other with pillows.

"Regressing," says my father indulgently.

"Not," I say, tickling my brother under his ribs.

"Stop that. Liza, stop!"

"Say uncle."

"Uncle."

"Hey, where's Gregor?" I ask my father.

"Your mother's showing him the garden," says my father. "Your brother brought some seeds from his journeys, and we've been planting them."

I mimic smoking a joint. "Hey Daniel, remember when you had that 'plant' in your room and you told Mommy it was for a science project?"

My brother rolls his eyes at me, indicating my father's presence, but he isn't even listening. My father puts his hand on my arm. "Liza, go outside and take a look at my new rocks."

My brother and I give each other a meaningful look. On

family vacations as far back as we can remember, my father would stop the car, weighing down our pea green station wagon with large rocks for his stone walls. He would even stop at other people's stone walls and pick up their strays. "It's not stealing," he would say. He considered that if other people made inferior walls, used any kind of adhesive to bind the rocks together, they weren't serious enough to deserve the stray rocks. In his stone walls, he would balance the rocks by sheer force of will.

When I get outside, I see Gregor and give him a playful punch.

He says, "Ow," and grabs his arm like I've mortally wounded him.

"Do you notice how she regresses when she comes up here?" says my mother to Gregor, confidentially.

He nods. "Liza, your mother was just showing me the garden. She's going to give me some cuttings."

"Well, you're going to have to take care of them. I have a black thumb."

I LEAVE GREGOR to charm my mother and walk in the other direction with my brother. This is the first time he's met Gregor.

"So Gregor seems nice," says Daniel, approvingly.

"Yeah, he's okay." I don't want to talk about Gregor, as if the moment I announce our relationship a success, it will fail.

"I heard about Bette and her new boyfriend. What's he like?"

"I only met him for two minutes. He is the brother of a guy I used to work with at that awful law firm. According to Bette, he's the second coming. So, how's your love life?"

"A bit of a dry spell at the moment."

"Did I tell you I quit my job?" I say, sitting down on the grass.

My brother looks surprised. "Did you tell them?"

"The parental units? No, not yet."

My brother sits gingerly on a wooden bench from IKEA that my father constructed with difficulty from the instruction book. He is still as thin as I remember but he looks entirely different than he did a few years ago. Five years ago my brother couldn't walk at all. He was in law school and he contracted a mysterious illness that attacked his joints. He went to doctor after doctor, took test after test. For a while, they thought he had chronic fatigue, then Lyme disease, then a connective tissue disorder. After traditional medicine gave up on him, he started going to alternative healers and now he only has occasional aches and pains, although I don't think my parents have ever forgiven him for dropping out of law school.

Daniel looks at me and I can see what his patients must find so comforting—that total attention and sympathy.

"I hated it, the job, I mean. I was so bored. I know I'm supposed to have some great career, but I have hated every real job I've ever had."

MY PARENTS MAKE us brunch. They want everything to be perfect. I want everything to be perfect. It's as if we all have this vision of the perfect family that we can never live up to. Gregor is the only one totally unconcerned.

On the wooden table, there is a wicker basket of bagels and bialys and pottery platters filled with smoked salmon, sliced tomatoes from the garden, and a variety of cream cheeses.

"Bagels and lox," says my father proudly, "but Liza, I got you some cheddar cheese to melt on your bagel."

"But I like smoked salmon," I say, annoyed.

My father shakes his head. "No, you don't."

"Dad, you're thinking of Bette," my brother tells him, but my father still looks unconvinced.

"We are separate people you know." I spear some lox on my fork and spread a defiant slice on my bialy.

Gregor smiles at me. He is eating contentedly. He loves Jewish food. He eats slower than the rest of us, putting lox, capers, onion and tomato into a careful construction while everyone else is almost finished with their first bagel.

My parents question Gregor about his acting career, his plans, and I feel my throat tighten thinking about my own lack of a plan. When Gregor finishes talking I announce to no one in particular, "I quit my job."

My parents look around alarmed, and my brother steps in, as I knew he would. He makes soothing noises. "Liza needs some time. She needs to figure out where she is going. Don't pressure her."

"But do you think she's doing the right thing?"

"I'm sure she doesn't have any savings."

"What about health insurance?"

It feels strange having them talk about me in the third person. Gregor doesn't say anything but he presses his knee against mine for support.

I feel a need to hear my own voice. "I couldn't deal with it anymore. And anyway, I've got a few part-time jobs, walking dogs, working in a café. And I'm getting unemployment."

"Well, if it makes you happy," my mother says doubtfully, "but you do need health insurance."

"I have Cobra right now, but when that runs out I'll have to deal with it." Cobra. Insurance. Snakes.

There is a long disapproving silence.

"Coffee?" says my mother brightly, changing the subject.

"It's real, it's not decaf, is it?" I ask suspiciously.

My mother tries to remember. "Yes I'm sure it's got caffeine, it was in the freezer. That coffee in the freezer is regular, right Harold, that's why we put it there?"

My father nods distractedly. "Does Bette hate all fish, or just lox?"

"All fish," I say, louder than I mean to. "She hates all fish. She always has."

"Interesting."

I BRING IN the chocolate cake I brought and we all sing "Happy Birthday." Gregor and I give my mother a pair of earrings. Daniel gives her a pottery thing, which at first we think is a vase, but then decide is a sculpture.

She kisses us, looking embarrassed and pleased.

After the cake is reduced to a few crumbs on our plates, I help my mother clean up.

In the kitchen, I ask my mother if she is still thinking about going to therapy, like her doctor suggested, to deal with the loss of her dream program, her impending retirement, the stress. She is sponging the Mexican tile counter, which, because of all the little nooks and crannies, never seems quite clean.

"I did go for a few times, but then she retired." She places the sponge definitively back on the edge of the sink, as if that is the end of the matter.

I pick up the sponge and get a spot she missed.

"Well, you could find someone else."

"Isn't it great about Bette meeting someone?" says my mother, ending our discussion.

"Yeah, great."

"She sent me flowers."

"They're pretty," I say, reaching down to smell a purple one.

"We went to see *The Seagull* with her last week and she was beaming."

124

GREGOR AND I are staying in the cottage, the little building that was once a garage, that my parents have converted into a guest cottage. When we get inside, I collapse onto the bed. It's always this way. The longer I stay at my parents', the more a sense of lethargy pervades me, as if the air is leaden with Quaaludes or Valium. I always imagine that I'll take long walks in the country, go into town, read all the books I bring, accomplish something, but when I get here I eat and sleep and barely can rouse myself from a lounge chair. If I stayed for more than a week, I'd probably end up in a coma. I wander around the room fingering the spines of books I loved as a child that have ended up stored in the cottage. *The Phantom Tollbooth*, *Charlotte's Web*, *The Little Princess*. I'd like to crawl inside one of those books for a while and just forget about my problems.

AFTER LUNCH, GREGOR goes for a run.

My brother does something in his room.

My parents work in the garden. I go over and look at them. They are engrossed in their separate activities. My father is working on a stone wall. My mother is busy also, weeding relentlessly in the hot sun, a fringed scarf wrapped around her head, making her at first glance look like Yasir Arafat. As I look around, I notice there are stone constructions I don't remember, little stone pathways, small stone hedges, the new wall my father's building near the house. Soon the whole yard will be encased in stone, like a castle.

"You've been doing a lot of work," I say.

My father nods. "That's what I do."

My parents have always tried to get me to garden, but the pleasure of it eludes me. I hate the feeling of the dirt under my fingernails, the heat, the bending over.

I sit in a battered lawn chair, take out my book of career exercises, and try to work on the section I had skipped over, the section entitled "Who Are You?" Good question. The first exercise is to think of a color. Then imagine you are inside that color. There are blanks in the book for the answer. I am the color _____. I am _____ and _____. OK, this should be easy. Colors. I look around me for ideas. My lawn chair is indeterminate beige. The grass is green, and I consider being green for a moment, but then I start to feel seasick. No, I am definitely not the color green. I try blue. But that makes me think of smoky nightclubs, where ancient men croon sad songs. There is only one color that I can be, I realize, looking down at my black dress. "I am black," I write in the blanks. I am black and absorb light. I am fashionable and mysterious and I camouflage dirt.

A shadow interrupts my flow of thought. I squint and look up. My father is standing over me.

I close my book and sit up. He sits down next to me.

He looks concerned. "So honey, are you okay? Do you need any money?"

"No, I'm fine." I push the thought of credit card bills out of my mind.

"So what are you reading?"

"*How to Be What You Could Have Been.*"

"How's it going?"

"Good."

"And have you found what you could have been yet?"

Looking up at my father's concern, I have to have an answer, so I say the first thing that pops into my head: "I'm going to write children's stories." It sounds strange to me, and I'm not sure why I said it.

My father looks surprised. "What about your poetry? Are you still writing? I always thought you had a talent for that . . ."

126

"I used to think I did too, but I can only write poetry when I'm deeply unhappy. I need a career that's more versatile."

"Well, it's a very competitive field. It won't be easy."

"I know that."

WHEN MY FATHER goes back to working on his unfinished stone wall, I take out my pad and start writing my first children's story, the first one I have ever attempted, or even thought of attempting. The title pours out of me like tears: *Liza the Reluctant Lemming.*

I write for a page without stopping. I write about Liza the Lemming who refuses to fall into the sea. She rebels and makes her way to New York City.

I stop when another shadow stands over me, Gregor, dripping, from his run.

He leans down and kisses me, "You okay?"

"Why shouldn't I be? Hey, do you know anything about lemmings?"

FOR THE REST of the day I feel a strange calm. I have a plan. This is what I'm going to do. Write a children's story. It is the first thing that feels right. I don't want to solve people's problems, be responsible for them, be a therapist or an astrologer. I am the color black. I want to help them escape.

AT DINNER, MY parents do not talk about my future. My brother has convinced them I am in a fragile state and we talk about movies, politics, friends of my parents and their ailments.

I LISTEN TO the conversation but my heart is with Liza the Lemming. She wears a bow in her hair and listens to alternative music. She is an orphan, alone in the world, but undefeated.

THE ONLY PERSON I want to tell about my new venture is my sister but she is the one person who is unavailable to me.

I used to call Bette three or four times a day, for contact, to ask small questions about food and wardrobe, but now when I call her, she sounds distracted, faraway, forgets my questions.

I don't tell my parents about Liza the Reluctant Lemming. I've found that when new ideas are exposed to the family atmosphere, they tend to shrivel up and die.

Chapter fourteen

SINCE GREGOR'S BEEN back from summer stock, it's like we're really living together for the first time. We've been cooking, trying to save money.

"What should we have for dinner?" I find myself asking him in the morning, before he rushes off to acting class, or singing class, or movement class.

But what do I really care about what we have for dinner? When we were first dating and teeming with pheromones, we didn't worry about dinner. When Gregor was away, I waited to see what I felt like eating. Now that we are living together, a couple, this horrible domestic script erupts out of my mouth. There seems to be some inverse ratio between sex and dinner. Lately it's been more dinner, less sex. Soon, I'll probably want to post a cleaning schedule on the fridge.

On weekend nights, we watch pay-per-view movies and eat one-pot meals like my mother used to make. All this heavy food is weighing me down, but I feel compelled. I cook huge vats of black bean chili, paella, nutritious, economical meals that make me want to scream.

"Our refrigerator looks like some futuristic planet," says Gregor, examining one of the tinfoil monstrosities. "What is this?"

"I don't know—Frozen Reynolds Wrap Surprise."

Gregor goes out to movement class, and I do the laundry, even Gregor's, folding each pair of his underwear carefully. His underwear is like that of a little boy, underwear with patterns, bikinis with little space ships, tartan plaid underwear. His underwear makes me feel safe and sleepy and I lie down on top of all the warm, clean underwear, suddenly exhausted.

I HAVE A dream about Jay McInerney, the author. I am in his hotel suite drinking champagne and he is telling me that he never made a penny from his writing. I tell him how much I loved his book *Story of My Life,* and he leans in close and tells me he wants to take a shower with me. He is wearing a large white hotel room towel and nothing else. In the dream, I am incredibly attracted to him but I know there is some reason I shouldn't sleep with him.

Peeling myself off the pile of laundry in a flurry of static, I get up from the bed. I go to the bookcase and look at the picture of Jay McInerney on the book jacket cover of his novel, *Bright Lights, Big City.* He has dark hair and eyes. He's OK-looking, but he doesn't do anything for me. He looked better in the dream. But, as my mother would say, "All characters in a dream are different aspects of yourself." He must be the writer part, the writer who wants to have a shower with the rest of me.

It's one of those dreams I wake from dazed, as if I have taken too many antihistamines. I want to crawl back into the dream and have sex with the dream Jay McInerney who is really a part of myself. With a huge effort, I propel myself to the kitchen and drink some coffee. I decide to work on my children's story, reading it over from the beginning.

Liza the Lemming was an orphan. She had been left as a baby lemming, a lemlet, in a wicker basket at the foot of the Central Norwegian Foundling Hospital. She didn't even have individual parents, instead she had a series of trainee parents, from the parent academy. She had no idea where she was from originally. She could have been from anywhere, even from New York.

"Liza, you're obsessed with New York," said her friend Sandor. "I thought I was different, and all I want is to go to Oslo and study ice sculpture."

When I start to write, I get nervous. I have to write quickly before I have time to think about it. I have been trying to write every day and I've discovered that within each day, there is a critical moment that determines whether I will get something written or get nothing written. It is the moment when I sit down at the kitchen table, with my purple writing notebook made in France and the special purple pen I bought with the fish that float up and down inside of it. If the phone rings, I am finished. Or if my closet calls out to me, "Organize me, organize me," I'm done for.

For me, being a writer involves a great deal of coffee, anxiety and self-doubt, and after a few good lines, elation. If I write, no matter how little—a sentence, an idea—I can breathe easy, go out and buy myself an instant Lotto ticket, sit in a café. If I don't write, I have to find some way to punish myself. Today is one of the days when I will not write. Liza the Lemming faces too many possibilities and I am unable to choose one.

I read the newspaper: war, violence, terrorism, cancer. I look in the jobs section but I still can't figure out which category I'm interested in. I call my bank and find out from an electronic voice that I have $126 in my checking account.

In the Living section of the paper, there's an article about

all the ingredients you should have on hand to cook an inex-
pensive impromptu meal and I start to write them down in my
purple notebook:

Pasta
Canned Italian plum tomatoes
Cayenne pepper
Extra virgin olive oil
Dried porcini mushrooms
Green-olive paste
Pesto
Anchovies

I decide to go out and go shopping, seized by a sudden
desire to cook.

I MAKE SPAGHETTI alla puttanesca from the recipe in the *Times*.
"Hooker's pasta," I tell Gregor, "you know from when the
Italian prostitutes used to sit around and make meals when
they didn't have any customers. It's an aphrodisiac."
He pushes me against the stove, mock-serious. "You know
how that kind of talk excites me."
My phone rings. "Should I get it?" I ask, hoping he'll say
no and drag me into the bedroom.
"Yeah, go ahead," says Gregor, a long strand of spaghetti
hanging from his mouth. I take the phone in the bedroom and
lie down on the bed while I talk.

"SO, WHO WAS it?" he asks me, when I get off the phone and
settle back on the couch with my bowl of pasta.
"Gwendolyn, the lady I walk the dog for. She strained her
back and they want me to put in some extra hours."
"I know you like them and everything, Liza, but wouldn't

you be better off getting a job with benefits that pays more than minimum wage?"

"Gregor, I'm going to pay you back that money I owe you."

"That's not what I'm talking about. I don't want that back. I think you need some security."

"*You* don't have security. Could you pass me the cheese?"

"But I have savings, and when I do work, I make good money."

"Don't worry about me, I'll be fine. Anyway, it's temporary, they need me."

I GO OVER TO Gwendolyn and Amelia's the next morning, not quite sure what's going to be expected of me, but glad for the distraction. It's not even ten o'clock and I know I won't be able to write a word about Liza the Lemming.

Obey, the dog, barks happily at my arrival, licking my hand.

"Bowling, of all things," says Amelia, shaking her head. "That's how she hurt herself. She only throws gutter balls anyway, so I don't know why she bothers."

"I heard that," Gwendolyn calls out from her bedroom down the hall.

"So what do you need me to do?" I glance around cautiously, imagining bedpans and sponge baths.

"Oh, a little of this and a little of that. If you could come in the mornings, let's say nine-thirtyish, and take care of walking the little monster, oh you know I'm talking about you don't you Obey"—Amelia pets the dog energetically—"then we'll see how it goes."

GWENDOLYN'S STRAINED BACK is a blessing for me. I come in the mornings and make cheese-and-pickle sandwiches for their lunch and huge pitchers of iced tea with mint. Amelia makes fudge or goes out for walks and I sit with Gwendolyn and talk, or read to her. She loves New Age magazines and anything about past lives. Sometimes we read tarot cards. Today she reads my palm.

"You have a very strong success line in your right hand, but not in your left," she tells me, shaking her head slightly.

"What does that mean?"

"That you haven't fully developed your potential."

"I could have told you that."

"Liza, you're doing exactly what you need to be doing, you just don't realize it yet."

MY LIFE IS so unlike the life I imagined I would have at thirty-two. I remember my mother's friends and how grown-up and important they seemed to me, sitting around the kitchen table in their peasant blouses talking about their jobs and their marriages and their sex lives. It's hard to believe they were my age, or younger. I wonder if I will ever feel grown up. Maybe it's easier to feel mature with all the proper accoutrements: kids, mortgage, husband, career. I remember sitting at the special kids table at the larger family events we used to go to. I liked sitting at the small wobbly table that never matched the height of the big table where the grown-ups were sitting. I think I still want to sit there.

GREGOR CONTINUES TO disapprove of my working at Gwendolyn and Amelia's. He is worried about my future. "What are you, some kind of home health aide?"

"No, I'm just there to keep them company. And Gwendolyn's teaching me how to do foot reflexology. She has a book."

All the Lemmings were excited about the trip planned for the night of the solstice. The trip, called the migration, hap-

pened once every fifty years. The Lemming Kings had issued an official proclamation and there was going to be a special banquet the night before. Liza was the only one who had questions. "Why are we going?" she asked anyone who she could find, but everyone shushed her. "And why are only the younger Lemmings going?" she asked the elders. "It's a tradition," said one of the Lemming Kings sternly. "This is what the overnight retreats have prepared you for. You will go south and seek out other Lemming tribes and join them." Liza thought the whole idea was ridiculous. Why should we move, and if we are going to move, why not go somewhere exciting like New York?

She talked to her teachers at school. They were kind but they just kept saying that it would be a wonderful learning experience. "You're lucky to be a part of the Migration," they said, as if they were envious. "We're too old to go," they said sadly. "It will be wonderful. You'll grow, as a lemming," they told her. "If I live through it," muttered Liza under her breath.

Gregor got a call from a casting agent. He is ecstatic. They want him to audition for *All My Children*, the soap opera my sister and I watched obsessively during high school summers, tracking every vicissitude of Pine Valley, every affair, every betrayal, every evil twin.

"They loved my English butler accent," he tells me, rushing in and out again to the audition.

WHEN GREGOR GETS home, I make a Greek chickpea stew from a recipe I clipped from a natural health magazine.

While it's simmering, I call my sister, although it's really her turn to call me.

"I have some news!" says my sister, sounding excited on the phone from Westchester, where she is now firmly ensconced.

"Spill!"

135

"We're moving to LA."

"Well, you think that's news, I've been cooking dinner!"

"No, I'm serious."

"So am I. How can you be serious? Nobody lives in LA."

"Well, Lawrence has this great job offer, designing pools. This really big design firm saw his pool in the Hamptons and offered to move him out to LA."

Just at the moment I decide to accept Lawrence and Bette as a couple, start imagining double-dating with them, begin to think it might be OK, things get pushed up a notch. Westchester is far enough, but LA is unimaginable. I knew Lawrence was some kind of architect or designer, but I didn't know he was looking for a job.

I hear my sister's voice faintly. ". . . It's a really good opportunity for Lawrence. Lawrence has friends out there . . . Lawrence says . . . Lawrence thinks . . ."

Lawrence, Lawrence Lawrence.

"I guess that's great! But LA? Why does it have to be so far?"

"I don't know if you know this, but they do have airplanes that can fly from New York to California. Remember when you lived in San Francisco and I flew out to visit you?"

"Once."

It's true. Bette came out to visit me when I lived with Charles. I remember it distinctly. She told me she didn't like the way he treated me, said he was too controlling and we had a huge fight on Fisherman's Wharf over large bowls of cioppino. Seeing my sister with Lawrence reminds me how deeply I sank into Charles's life, two years of my life disappearing without a trace.

"What are you going to do out there, what about your research, your teaching, your dissertation?"

"It can wait, it's beginning to seem so pointless to me, anyway, analyzing literature."

136

"It's not pointless. It's important, and you've done so much work. I don't know how you could give up your work on toast."

"I'm not giving it up, I'm only taking a break."

"Whatever. So, when do you want to get together, Saturday?"

"No, we're really busy, making plans, getting ready. It's funny, I just moved out here to Westchester and here I'll have to start packing again."

"Don't you think it's a little sudden?"

"Liza, you wanted me to be in a relationship. You should be excited for me."

"I am. I'm just in a state of shock. Are you sure you don't want to go see a movie or something, maybe Sunday?"

"I'll call you."

When I get off the phone, I turn to Gregor.

"Bette's moving to LA!!!"

"You're kidding."

"I wish I was."

"When?"

"I don't know. Soon."

Gregor's phone rings. I rush up to get it, thinking it's Bette and she's changed her mind, that she wants to get together, but it's someone asking for Gregor.

I walk in my bedroom and start arranging the objects on my dresser. This is something I do when I'm upset. I separate the earrings into different little jewelry boxes, studs in one, dangling earrings in another. I arrange all the makeup, sharpen my eye pencils, put all the pennies in the special change cup. I can't believe Bette is really leaving.

Gregor pops his head in the door while I'm wiping all the spilled face powder off the wood.

137

"I got it!" says Gregor, the phone still in his hand.

"What? The part? *All My Children?*"

He grabs me around the waist. "I can't believe it Liza, I actually got it." He looks so happy, I feel happy. The phone cord wraps around both of us and we whirl around trying to untangle it.

"That's great, honey, that's incredible. Who are you?"

"I am the mysterious English lord."

"So, when do you start, when are you going to be on? When are we going to go to the Emmys?"

"We start shooting Monday. But I'm only a noncontract day player, so I could be on just for a couple of days, so we can't get too excited."

"They'll want to keep you once they see you."

WE GO OUT for dessert. I put on my leopard-print dress.

"Gregor, do you think this dress is getting a little tight?" I twist around to try to see my backside in the mirror. When I see it, I decide to cut out the late-morning shortbread cookies at Gwendolyn and Amelia's.

Gregor takes a long time to respond.

"Well?"

He looks me deep in the eyes. "You look beautiful."

"Well, you're an actor. I can't trust what you say."

OVER NAPOLEONS WITH whipped cream at the Hungarian Pastry Shop, I start to despair. I should be happy for Gregor. I am happy for Gregor but I wish I knew that writing was what I was meant to be doing. I wish I could be sure. I wish Bette weren't moving to LA. I wish I hadn't gained weight.

I don't want to ruin Gregor's celebration, but I can't help myself. "Maybe I shouldn't be writing children's books. It's not like I ever wanted children, or know anything about them."

"Liza, you worry too much. It'll be fine."

"Maybe I should get a real job, quit working at the café and walking the dogs."

"You had a real job and you hated it."

"A legal secretary is not a real job, it's a nightmare. Anyway, the other day you were telling me I needed security."

"Well you do, both things are true. You need security and you'd hate a real job."

"Look, let's not talk about this now, we're supposed to be celebrating your thing anyway. Let's get more cappuccinos."

*M*Y PARENTS HAVE us all over for a good-bye dinner at their apartment in the City. They want to see us all together before Bette moves to Los Angeles. My parents are excited about Gregor's part in the soap opera and Lawrence's new job with designer pools. It's as if Gregor and Lawrence are the successful children they wish they had. Surprisingly, my parents don't seem to disapprove of my sister taking a leave of absence from teaching; in fact, they seem to encourage it. My mother says something vague about distance giving you clarity. They probably figure Bette is getting some higher degree in coupledom. I shouldn't blame them. Bette is probably their only hope for grandchildren. I would like my parents to have grandchildren, but not from my body.

"COULDN'T YOU TEACH out there?" I ask her, during a pause in the conversation.

"I suppose," says my sister, "I'll have to see."

My parents plan a visit to LA to see my sister. A former student from my mother's dream program lives out there so they'll stay with her.

"We'll have to go after we get back from Bali."

Everyone starts talking about Bali.

Lawrence says the dance and crafts are great, if too commercialized.

My sister asks if they are going to stop in Hawaii on the way out.

Gregor says he's always wanted to go to Indonesia.

"But you're going to be gone for winter solstice!" I say.

"Well, everyone will be so scattered," shrugs my father.

My parents both seem happy about this scattering of the family over various continents, as if it is something they have been planning.

MY MOTHER SERVES us chilled zucchini soup in large earthenware bowls.

Gregor and Lawrence think it's delicious.

"Liza, what's wrong with you? You're not eating yours."

"I don't like cold soups, I never have. Remember how you would always have gazpacho and I would never eat it?"

I notice Bette playing with her soup. I roll my eyes at her but she ignores me and pretends she's eating it. She and Lawrence have their arms intertwined, even while they are eating the soup. It's as if there is some invisible force field that keeps them in physical contact at all times.

My parents are talking about LA. Lawrence is talking about his ideas for pools. Apparently Julia Roberts had one done in the shape of her dog.

"Who is Julia Roberts?" asks my mother.

"You know, Barbara," says my father, "she was in that movie with that Buddhist fellow, *Beautiful Lady*."

"*Pretty Woman*, Dad," I sigh. "*Pretty Woman*."

"Oh right," says my mother, "that was terrible."

OR THE MAIN course, we have steak.

"I'm thinking about becoming a vegetarian," I say to no one in particular.

"Don't be ridiculous, Liza," says my father. "You need your protein."

Over dessert, my mother hovers over my plate with the ladle. "Liza, are you sure you want more chocolate mousse?"

"Yes, I'm sure," I say defiantly.

MY PARENTS GIVE me and Gregor a ride home. I ask my parents how long they are staying in the City.

"We're driving back tomorrow. We just came down for the unveiling and to see you and your sister."

"Whose unveiling?"

"Remember your cousin Leah? Well, it's her father, he died a year ago, lung cancer."

"She probably never met him, Harold, she was too young," says my mother.

"Where do you have to go?" I ask.

"Out in Long Island. The Workmen's Circle Cemetery. We have a family plot."

"What do you mean, for us, our family? For me too?"

"Yes," my father tells me proudly. "There are spaces for all of us."

BEFORE I GO to sleep, I tell Gregor I want to go out there, to see the plot.

"Maybe we could have a picnic at the cemetery? I like cemeteries, did you know that?"

"You're crazy."

"Maybe you could be buried there too. You could be next to me."

"They probably wouldn't let me, because I'm not Jewish."

"I'm sure it's some socialist kind of plot, where they have to let everyone in, except Republicans."

I NEED FEEDBACK ON my writing so I decide to take a writing class at the New School. It's called "Writing from the Child Within." I can't afford it so I put it on the new Visa card I got in the mail. I arrive early and try to get comfortable in one of the right-handed chairs, as comfortable as is possible for a left-handed person in a right-handed chair. I look around to see what the average children's writer looks like. There is only one who seems the type, a grandmotherly woman who smiles and nods at everyone and looks like she should be knitting a sweater. The others make up an eclectic group, a guy with a mohawk, a girl who looks like a model, the rest an assortment of mainstream New York types.

MY WRITING CLASS meets once a week in a small classroom. We sit in a circle and the teacher makes us read our stories out loud. I feel a bond with the other writers. We are trying, however badly, to become something slightly bigger than ourselves. The first time I read my story out loud, my voice shakes. When I finish there is a silence that lasts forever. And then to my surprise, they seem to like it. The guy with the mohawk says it's funny. Somebody else says it's touching. They ask me why lemmings? I have no idea.

Liza smuggled herself onto a cruise ship, the night before the migration. Her seventh-grade class had gone down to the port to see the huge ship as part of a segment in social studies class. During the tour she slid under a deck chair and hid. She knew that in the mass confusion and excitement about the migration, she might not be noticed until it was too late. Just to make sure, she casually mentioned to Selma, a gossipy classmate, that she wasn't feeling well, and might have to go back home. "Bad herring," Liza told her, confidentially, holding her stomach. "Don't tell anyone. I'd hate to miss the banquet."

Chapter fifteen

MY SISTER IS far away, in Beverly Hills. She calls me frequently but doesn't seem to be able to grasp the time change so we end up missing each other. She leaves messages. What I gather from the answering machine is that the pool business is going well and Lawrence showers her with credit cards, a cell phone and a laptop computer.

I READ SOMEWHERE that after birth and death, the three most stressful events in life are moving, starting a new job and beginning a new relationship, but my sister acquired Lawrence, moved to LA and dispensed with her career as if *stress* were not a word in her vocabulary. It happened so quickly. Her move. First to Westchester, now to Los Angeles. Even their belongings were whisked away by specially trained movers and packers paid for by Splash, Lawrence's new company.

"At first I was embarrassed," Bette told me before she left, "to see these guys go through all my things. I thought that I was being lazy, but then I relaxed and it was wonderful."

Dear Bette,

How are you? I'm fine. Still working for the ladies with the dog, which is good because I can't borrow any more money from Gregor and my unemployment will run out in a couple of months. I've been reading articles on how to live on next-to-nothing, I have one here called the *Cheapskate Gazette*. Did you know that you can clean your entire house with white vinegar and baking soda? Unbelievable. For the first time in my life I've started to clip coupons. I haven't used them yet, but I feel very virtuous clipping them.

P.S. say hi to Lawrence.

P.P.S. Use no. 15 sunblock and wear a hat.

Your sister,

Liza

I write Bette postcards and every few days she calls me on her cell phone. She's made a new friend named Miranda, who lives next door. She sounds horrible. When I'm not home, Bette leaves me messages about which celebrity she and Miranda have seen.

We saw Meg Ryan! At the drugstore. I don't know what she was getting but Miranda said she looked terrible. How's the children's book coming?

Melanie Griffith, those lips. How could someone do that to themselves?

Sharon Stone, at Book Soup. She was signing her new book of poetry.

Gregor starts shooting this week for his part on *All My Children*. Apparently, Lord Haines is an eccentric Englishman who

146

has come to Pine Valley for mysterious reasons. He is nervous and excited and gets to wear lots of outrageous costumes.

MY SISTER IS in LA with Lawrence who dotes on the whims of celebrities and Hollywood executives.

I WALK A dog, work in a café and try to write. I want the writing to be the answer to all my problems but I don't think it can be.

MY SISTER HAS lost the use of her personal pronouns. She no longer says *I*, only *we* in her messages. *We liked that movie. We love LA. We love this great little restaurant on the coast for lunch.* I imagine my sister and Lawrence faraway, floating in space, totally enclosed like an egg.

My parents are a unit too, each incomplete without the other. I tried to be a unit once with Charles, moving into his condo in San Francisco, drinking chardonnay at business dinners with boring investment people from his firm, but I would drink too much and end up saying something shocking, like I didn't believe in capital punishment or I thought football was stupid.

MY SISTER IS safe in her egg, but I am suspicious. I remember in middle school, they taught us the salad bowl theory, that all the different nationalities should come to the United States and live in harmony, but retain their own identities, like all the ingredients in a salad bowl. Gregor and I are a salad. Bette and Lawrence are inside an egg.

Dear Bette,
It's been raining here, raining and cold. You're probably eating lunch al fresco at the pool and getting a tan.

I'm going to send you sections of my book like you asked. I haven't shown it to anyone yet, so be gentle.

147

Remember this is only a first attempt and Liza the Lemming is very sensitive to criticism. My class says the reading level of the story is too high. What do you think?

Love L

Liza the Lemming made her solitary way along the beach. She wasn't sure where she was, but given the festive atmosphere and profusion of men in pastel bikinis she supposed it must be Fire Island *which she had read about in the* Human Encyclopedia. *Liza rolled around on the beach, warming her fur on the sand. Humans with children were all around her. Some of the children tried to catch her but she was faster and smarter. The human parents didn't seem to notice her. They were too caught up in watching the human children. One child, a little girl named Tiffany, talked to Liza.*

"Hi, my name is Tiffany."

"I'm Liza."

"We're on vacation," said the little girl. "I ate two snowballs and a half pound of fudge and my brother has a boogie board."

"Thrilling," said Liza.

"Tiffany, Tiffany, what are you doing??? Come back here!!"

These techniques humans have for rearing their children leave something to be desired, thought Liza. I thought lemlets were treated badly. At least we are allowed some independence, allowed to go on overnight retreats. How else would we learn to fend for ourselves in the cold, cruel world? But I'm glad the world isn't so cold as I imagined, thought Liza, luxuriating in the velvet sand.

WHEN GREGOR COMES home, he enters cautiously, not sure what mood he will find me in. If I am drinking tea in the living room, good. Cleaning out my closet, bad. Writing, Very Good. Entering numbers on the calculator, Very Bad. Today, I am lying on the couch and reading the most recent issue of *Vogue*.

"I hate shawls," I tell Gregor.

He leans down and kisses me hello.

"How's Pine Valley?"

"Exhausting!"

"Did you have any love scenes?"

" Just one. They're not sure if they're going to use it."

"Did you kiss her?"

"Yes."

"Show me how you did it."

Gregor lies on the couch next to me, looks deep into my eyes and grabs me.

"Like this."

Without warning, he sticks his tongue in my mouth.

I pull away, laughing in surprise. "You do not!"

"No, of course not. It's pretty boring actually. The girl I'm involved with is a real chatterbox. She never shuts up."

"Oh, you poor thing, kissing for a living."

I imagine Gregor's job to be very glamorous with everyone calling each other "darling" all the time. He tells me it isn't.

"When we go to eat, we're all together in this big cafeteria, and there are these special people waiting by the door holding out these white paper smocks so we don't ruin our costumes."

"Even the big stars?"

"Everybody. It's like eating in a high school cafeteria. Chicken à la king, stuff like that."

"I love chicken à la king."

GREGOR IS ON the set from early in the morning till late at night. It's a good thing I'm working at Amelia and Gwendolyn's because otherwise I'm sure the minute Gregor was out the door I would crawl back into bed and stay there. Unfortunately, Gwendolyn's feeling better and they may not need me too much longer.

GREGOR WANTS TO pay the rent for a couple of months because he's making good money from the soap opera.

"No, I don't feel comfortable with that."

"Okay, how about you take your income and divide it into mine, and you can pay a pro rata share."

For some reason, I agree.

NOW THAT BETTE'S gone I feel an even greater need to figure out what I'm doing.

With my two extremely part-time jobs, I'm barely making enough money to live on and I have no prospects. Even with the new rent arrangement and buying absolutely nothing, I still need a job. No, I need a career. Something I can go to every day and not feel ashamed. And I need new shoes.

GWENDOLYN READS MY cards.

"There are a lot of cups. Emotions. See this card, the five of cups?" She points to a dark figure surrounded by goblets spilling red liquid on the ground.

"See the three cups on the ground? They represent disappointment but two cups are still standing. You have to focus on the future but something from the past is blocking you."

"My whole past is blocking me."

"But your past is also the answer to the future."

"I hate it when you're cryptic."

WHEN I GET home, I watch *All My Children* on my miniature TV. I eat lunch in the bathtub and wait for Gregor to appear. He's not on till the very end. I eat fruit and cheese, nothing with crumbs. It's odd to watch Gregor on the TV. It's like seeing his evil twin. When I see him kissing the girl, I don't feel anything, because I don't really believe it's him.

I TAKE OUT my career book again and do the exercises I skipped over the first time.

Imagine your perfect day and your perfect job.

OK, I'd wake up with Gregor; maybe we'd have a dog who would nuzzle up to us. Gregor would let the dog out and I'd make the coffee and bring it back to bed and we'd talk. Then I'd get dressed in a very flattering black outfit from my perfectly arranged closet and I would go into my office. My office would be near other people, but separate. What would I be doing in it? Writing. No, I like to write in cafés or in bed. And how do I know I have more than one children's story in me. Astrology? No, that's another thing I did because I liked it but if I tried to turn it into a job, I would lose interest. I like trying to figure people out, but I hate predicting their future.

And I still can't imagine a thing for mine.

Liza swam farther down the ocean, avoiding surfers and boogie boarders. She missed Sandor and even the orphanage. It would be snacktime around now.

Liza wandered into a wooden building on the beach. Loud music was making the entire structure vibrate. She walked up to the bar, boosted herself up on a crate and said in her best American English, "Coke please."

"Hey Ron, check this out. What are you?"

"What do I look like?"

"A large mouse?"

Liza couldn't believe this, a mouse indeed. She turned to go, but was stopped by a man's voice.

"He's got attitude."

"I'm a girl. A girl lemming. A Norwegian lemming from the Latin Lemmus."

"Why didn't you say so?"

"I just did."

"Buy this girl a Coke."

I start working and I am suddenly assailed by a chorus of voices. A chorus of evil little gnomes inside my head. *What makes you think you can be a writer? This plot is ridiculous. If you had started writing when you were twenty you would have published twelve novels by now instead of starting one measly little children's story.*

There is also a voice that says: Wouldn't it be really nice to have a nap right now?

I WAKE UP in the middle of the night in a panic. This is my life. And I have to do something about it before it's too late. Everything I have done before is wrong and I have to make it right. Gregor wakes up and tells me not to worry, that everything is going to be OK. He goes to the kitchen and gets me a glass of water.

"Here, drink this."

I sip on my water, feeling like Alice in Wonderland.

Later, I go into the bathroom and look at the spider veins on my thighs under the bright lights. The spiky purple lines seem indicative of my inevitable disintegration and death without ever having accomplished anything. I put on a new vitamin K cream I got at the Vitamin Shop and wait for all my problems to disappear.

"YOU SHOULD CALL people," says Gregor in the morning. "Don't stay in the house all day. You're too isolated."

"It's almost winter, I'm hibernating."

MAYBE GREGOR'S RIGHT. I'm too isolated and it's making me melancholy. I try calling my brother at the number he gave me, a drugstore in the tiny Costa Rican town where he's staying, but the man who answers the phone seems to have no knowledge of my brother. I begin to wish I had taken Spanish and not French in high school.

I CALL AN old friend from high school whom I haven't talked to in a few years. Andrea's a doctor. She lives in a very exclusive section of Chicago. She seems happy to hear from me and we discuss our friend Elinor who keeps in touch with both of us, and how she has to stop dating married men.

"I try to talk to her," I say, "but you know what she's like."

"Yeah, I know. Listen, you should come visit," she tells me. "You and Gregor."

Although we're the same age, Andrea is a grown-up. She has a house. A husband. Kids.

"So when are you two getting married, anyway?"

"I don't know, I'm not sure we believe in it."

"Oh," she sounds disappointed, and I try to reassure her.

"Well, we could change our minds."

I CALL MY friend Elinor. Before, I hardly ever used to call her, but since my sister's gone, we've been talking more frequently.

"So, I like this new guy," she tells me.

"Married?"

"Separated."

"Married."

"He's very nice."

"Well, you know what I think."

"You and my therapist. You both say the exact same things."

"Hey El, could you see me as a therapist?"

"I've always thought you'd be good at that. Ever since we were in abnormal psychology class together."

"But I don't see myself as the authority figure, the one people go to."

"You'd get over that."

"You really think I'd be good?"

"How many times do I have to say it?"

"Come on, please."

"Look, I've gone to more shrinks that I can count, and you'd be better than ninety-five percent of them."

"But . . ."

"You'd be fine."

"You sound like Gregor."

"Well, maybe you should listen to Gregor."

AT BARNES & Noble, I find a guide to careers in psychology and I feel the same dark feeling I had in college. I thumb through the book. Essays. GREs. Recommendations. Isn't it too late? I start to feel hot and dizzy and lean against the bookshelf, which sways slightly. I'm thirty-two. How can I do this now?

WHEN I GET home, there is a message on my machine from my parents, who have just returned from Bali.

I call them back.

"Hi Dad."

"We're so proud of Gregor."

"Yeah he's good, isn't he? Have you heard from Bette?"

"Yes, she seems to be settling in nicely."

"It's frightening."

"Liza, don't be so cynical. You should be happy for your sister."

"I am. I am." I walk around the kitchen arranging the spices in the kitchen in alphabetical order, cayenne, ginger, oregano, while my father tells me about Bali and dancers and artifacts and strange foods. Once the sociological analysis winds down, I ask him: "Hey Dad, what do you think of psychology?"

"As a subject or a career?"

"As a career, for me."

"I thought you were writing a children's story?"

MY CAREER BOOK says that people replay messages they have heard as a child. One assignment is to write down these messages and try to decipher them and how they've affected you. I read this, and one particular story of my father's keeps echoing in my head. He was drafted and served briefly in the army when he was in his early twenties, and he was particularly proud of the system he developed for dealing with basic training,

Most recently, he told us about it again at Bette's good-bye dinner.

"You take a bunk in the very middle of the barracks. A barracks is a long room with many cots, Liza."

"I know what a barracks is, Dad!"

"Okay, you put your gear down, and then you disappear. You go to the library, or the gym, stay there all day, don't talk to anyone, and when they come around to pick people for various tasks, they'll never even know you've been gone."

"You hide."

"No, you manipulate a situation to your advantage."

155

ON MY WAY to work, I buy an instant Lotto ticket and a Kit Kat. I decide that if I win any money, I will become a psychologist. I scratch off the symbols on my Lucky Stars card, one black hole, one lunar probe, one moon and one comet. If I get a black hole, I win ten thousand dollars. My last scratch reveals a moon. Well, I could do two out of three.

"MAYBE YOU SHOULD try psychic healing," says Gwendolyn, "you're very perceptive."

"You know, working with vibrations and auras," chimes in Amelia.

"Like that Louise Hay, she makes big bucks," says Gwendolyn.

"She's not doing it for the money, Gwennie."

The dog barks as if in agreement and we settle down to play hearts and eat shortbread cookies.

I DID SEE an aura once; at least I thought I did. My parents took me to an aura party at their friends', the Voltoffs. We all wore these funny plastic glasses, and I did see weird fuzzy outlines around people's heads but no one believed I had seen anything so I started to believe I hadn't.

WHEN I GET home it's dark and quiet. Gregor's probably out at one of his endless tapings. I consider cooking something but decide it's too much trouble.

I wander around the apartment aimlessly rearranging things, the vitamins, the CDs, my earrings. Gregor's desk is a mess, papers everywhere, scripts, notes, cards, indecipherable

Post-its. The light on his phone is blinking. I press the play button and turn the volume up.

There is a voice that sounds familiar on the phone, a southern voice. I have always hated southern accents. They sound so phony. But this woman is saying something about her and Gregor and the other night. In that syrupy southern accent. How he was great. In bed. The way she says it makes it sound like two words, *bay-yed*, and I have to focus to understand the word. I turn the machine off in mid-drawl.

I start arranging the papers on his desk into neat piles. Cards. Letters. Scripts. I remove all the Post-its and stack them up in a pile. I see an envelope from American Airlines and I take out a coupon for a free flight anywhere in the United States. I call the number and ask about today's flights to Los Angeles.

IN THE TAXI to the airport, the driver keeps asking me if I'm OK. I'm crying but I don't really feel anything. He gives me a pack of tissues.

"I'm fine," I say. "I've had a shock. A death in the family."

"Oh. I'm so sorry." He plays classical music for the whole ride to La Guardia.

"AISLE OR WINDOW?" the woman at the gate asks me, and I remember who the voice on the phone belongs to: the new segment producer on Gregor's show. He complained about her. How she has long red nails and big hair and is always firing everyone.

As I go through the metal detectors, I hate him so much I feel I might explode the whole device.

Chapter Sixteen

MY SISTER AND I have lunch in a Polynesian restaurant. The restaurant is a combination of cold metal furniture and gaudy Hawaiian prints. The chairs are uncomfortable and all the food tastes slightly wrong.

When I called Bette from the airport, she sounded distracted. I told her I needed a change of scene and my frequent flyer miles were about to expire. She said fine, she's been wanting me to visit anyway. She must know something's wrong, but so far, she hasn't asked me.

"A far cry from New York and the Mansion Diner," says my sister, as if she's proud of it.

"Yeah, it's wild." I don't say what I really think or feel. I am on alien territory and I have to be careful. I don't want to slip and tell my sister about Gregor. I dig my fingernail into my palm and try to act happy.

"I do miss those french fries."

"This is probably much healthier." I bite into what looks like an eggroll and tastes like pineapple. I hate pineapple. I hate LA. I hate Gregor.

"I have some good news," says my sister. She is wearing a sleeveless white dress and she has highlighted her hair. I keep staring at her arms. They are suddenly muscular. They look as if they couldn't have come from the same gene pool as mine.

"I'm not sure I can take any more good news," I say, fiddling with the parasol in my drink. All my sister's good news: falling in love with Lawrence, moving to Westchester and now LA, has not come at a good time for me.

My sister smiles and says, "I'm having a baby."

I choke on my mango champagne cocktail.

"Now don't freak out, Liza, but I'm going to have it."

"Why would I freak out?"

"Because you hate children."

"I don't hate them. I'm maternally challenged." It's true: From as early as I can remember thinking about it, I have been totally opposed to the notion of procreation. Maybe I saw too many science fiction movies as a child, but it always seemed fundamentally unnatural to me, to have something growing inside you, sapping your strength for nine months only to tear its way out. I look at my sister more carefully, as if I will be able to detect some new maternal quality.

"So, what do you think?"

"You're pregnant," I say slowly. For some strange reason, I am happy about this. Now I don't have to go through this, my sister will do it for both of us. I feel a need to do something. I reach up and we hug awkwardly over our metal table. Spontaneous hugging is not done in my family, but I do it before I have a chance to restrain myself.

I blink back emotion and sit back down. "Congratulations."

"I'm glad you're happy. I know how you feel about children."

"I am happy for you. Really." I start crying, seriously crying, and I grab my napkin and press it against my eyes.

160

My sister looks at me, confused.

I blurt out, "Gregor is having an affair."

"What!"

"I'm sorry, I know we should be talking about you, and I *am* happy really, about the baby, but I don't know what to do."

"Are you sure?"

"There was a message on his machine. I listened to it. I don't know why, but I turned up the volume and listened to it. From his producer on the soap. She said she had a great time the other night. That he was great. In bed. She actually said that. I can't believe it. It's so clichéd and ridiculous. And you've moved out here and you're I don't know different and I can't talk to you anymore and I hate this food and this restaurant and LA. Do you have a tissue?"

"Oh, Liza, I'm sorry. I didn't know."

LATER, WE SIT by the pool in the back of their ultramodern white house. My sister tells me the pool Lawrence designed in the Hamptons is going to be shown in *InStyle* magazine. She tells me the pool is in the shape of a question mark and the dot is a separate hot tub. That the company rented them this house. Lawrence's accomplishments have taken the place of her accomplishments.

Lawrence is treating Bette like she is a priceless object, a Fabergé egg. He keeps giving her inflatable cushions.

"You're going to smother her," I tell him.

They drag me into their hot tub. I don't feel comfortable. My skin is so white and the water is moving too much.

"This is great, isn't it?" says Lawrence.

"Yeah, but do you think it's safe? I mean there all those hot wet germs floating around," I say, unable to stop myself.

Bette and Lawrence both laugh indulgently, as if I am insane. Bette says to Lawrence, "She's always been like this, when she was little, she would refuse to open the windows in

161

her room at night, even when it was a hundred degrees out!"

"Well, things could have gotten in," I say, defending myself.

I MADE BETTE promise not to tell Lawrence but I still feel like he knows. He keeps leaving us alone.

I try to act normal until Lawrence goes into the house.

"I knew when I moved in we shouldn't have gotten separate phone lines. It was a mistake. This never would have happened if we had shared the same phone. If he had wanted to share the same phone. He said it was because of his career, but I think it was because he never really loved me."

My sister looks pained at the idea of love evaporating. "I'm sure he still loves you, Liza, this is probably some misunderstanding."

"Right."

"Do you want a drink?"

"Sure, I might as well become an alcoholic now."

My sister goes into the kitchen and brings back a margarita for me and a seltzer for herself.

"I think you and Gregor should try to work this out."

T HE PHONE RINGS while I'm on my second margarita.

"It's Gregor," says my sister with her hand over the receiver. "He wants to talk to you."

My stomach does internal gymnastics. I whisper, "I can't."

Bette doesn't miss a beat. "Gregor, she's in the shower," my sister says in her frosty professorial voice, the voice she would use with an undergraduate who had some lame excuse why their paper was late.

I CAN'T BELIEVE he could do it. Be with someone else. Every time I think about it I start crying. My tears are mingling with the hot germ-laden water in the hot tub. I'm such an idiot. I thought things were going so well. It was the one area of my life I wasn't worried about. He'd been so nice lately. But it's like they say in those *Cosmo* articles I used to read, all those late nights, the niceness, all the signs were there.

"Liza he wants you to call him back. He's very insistent."

"I can't." I watch the skin on my fingers shrivel up.

"You're going to have to talk to him eventually. What are you going to do?"

"I don't know. I feel embarrassed."

"Why?"

"That I should have known or something. I thought if I could decide on a career, everything would be okay. Some psychologist I would make, I don't even know that my own boyfriend is having an affair."

"You don't know that it's an affair."

"Whatever it is, it's bad."

"You know, you can stay here as long as you want."

"No, you don't want a houseguest."

"Don't be an idiot."

"Bette, I missed you."

"Me too. Nobody here reads anything."

"Speaking of that, what are you going to do about your work? You can't abandon Barbara Pym and Angela Thirkell."

"I know. I do miss it, but I was just so sick of all the infighting in the department. I just wanted to be left alone to do my research."

"You could still do work here, right?"

"I want to enjoy life for a while. My whole adult life, I've always been in school, one way or the other."

"Wasn't it what you wanted?"

"I'm not sure I thought I had a choice. It's different being the oldest, there was more pressure on me."

LAWRENCE STICKS HIS head out of the screen door and announces dinner.

"He knows doesn't he?"

My sister shrugs. "I couldn't help it."

"Well at least I don't have to pretend I have allergies," I say, sniffing into a tissue.

TWO WEEKS GO by. Gregor calls the house at regular intervals. I don't talk to him but I feel strangely comforted by the twinkling lights on my sister's answering machine.

ONE DAY, THE phone rings and I pick it up. It's a portable and I hold it slightly away from my mouth, as if I am afraid of catching something.

"Liza, I've been trying to call you. Are you okay?"

The sound of his voice hurts my ears. I interrupt him. "I'm staying here for a while, in LA, with Bette. My sister's expecting."

"Expecting what?"

"A baby. She's having a baby."

"Is that good?"

"Yes, it's good, of course it's good."

"Liza, what's the matter, you sound weird. Why did you take off like that? What's wrong?"

Don't say anything. Don't tell him you know.

"Look Gregor, I know. All right? So let's stop this . . . this pretense of a relationship."

"Stop what? . . . I can hardly hear you, is there something wrong with your phone?" It's so awful to hear Gregor's voice and not tell him what I'm thinking, not confide in him about this horrible thing that's happened to me.

I put my mouth close to the receiver: "I know, okay, I know about you, and that woman, in the hotel. I listened to the message on your answering machine. So, I know why you didn't want to move in with me, that you don't . . ." I will not cry. I will not cry. I bite down hard on the inside of my mouth.

"Liza, I did want to move in with you and this doesn't . . . it's not . . . please come back to New York. We need to talk."

I hear his words, but I don't feel anything, only anger. "There's nothing to talk about. I would appreciate it if you would forward my mail."

I click off the phone and stare at it.

*T*HE NEXT DAY my sister and I go to a cemetery. Cemeteries calm me down. Cemeteries and supermarkets.

"Bette, do you think it's serious? This thing? Between Gregor and his producer?"

"No. For all you know it was a one-night stand. Maybe she made him, to keep his job."

"Yeah, right. You know I saw her once, when I picked Gregor up at the soap opera. She's older than us. A lot older. And she wears those stupid pastel kind of suits and chunky gold jewelry. How could he?"

WE SIT AT a bench in front of Marilyn Monroe's crypt. There are fresh lipstick marks over her name.

"Do you think someone comes by every day and kisses her?" asks my sister. "It's kind of sweet."

"Yeah, probably some drag queen."

Bette's face grows concerned. "Liza, do you really think I'm different, that I've changed?"

I have to be careful here. "Well, I don't know, you were acting weird for a while, but now you seem more like yourself."

W E WALK AROUND the cemetery, stopping at a memorial to a little girl named Edith. There is a statue of her in a round glass case. She has Shirley Temple curls and is wearing a frilly dress carved in stone. I lie on the grass next to Edith and stretch my arms and legs out.

"What are you going to name her?"

"Jane, I think it's going to be a girl too."

"For Jane Austen?"

"It seems like a sturdy intelligent name."

"She'll probably complain about it later."

"I know, isn't it odd to think of purposefully bringing someone into the world who is genetically programmed to hate you by the time they reach adolescence."

"You'll probably be one of those sickening mother and daughters who actually like each other."

"I hope so."

AFTER THE CEMETERY, we drive around and my sister points out different sights, the La Brea Tar Pits, the Hollywood Bowl, various celebrity homes. My sister, it turns out, isn't so crazy about LA, but the neon and glitter are perfect for my disoriented state. I make her stop at a drive through with a huge pink neon sign spelling DOGS.

I order a bacon chili cheese dog with onions. Although we ate lunch only a few hours ago, I am ravenous and the hot dog is delicious.

166

"Liza, I thought you were becoming a vegetarian."

"Desperate times call for desperate measures."

As we get back into her car, a white jeeplike vehicle, I contemplate living here.

"You know, if I did want to stay here, I'd have to get a job, a real job."

"Maybe Lawrence could help, he knows a lot of people."

I SLEEP IN the "loft," a small room at the top of the house with a tiny round window. The longing to call Gregor is so strong my fingertips itch. I control it by thinking of him with the producer lady. For some reason, I see him in his Lord Haines costume, fully dressed, having sex with her. She is totally naked, and they are on the leather couch in her office. He only unbuttons his pants, keeping his long velvet jacket and frilly poet shirt on.

It's warm out, but I cover myself with all the blankets I can find. I feel sleepy from the food and the wine at dinner. I decide to stay in LA. I will have a new life here. A Gregor-less life. I will get involved with a famous director and when Gregor tries out for a part, we will crush his career like a bug. I will go to the Oscars and sweep by Gregor, who will be parking cars, in my stunning Christian Dior ball gown.

I go to sleep and dream of twins with long red hair.

"BREAKFAST?" ASKS MY sister when I stumble downstairs the next morning.

The thought of food makes me feel ill. "No thanks."

I get some orange juice from the see-through refrigerator and make some ice cubes from the automatic ice-cube maker. I fish out one of the cubes and press it against my forehead.

"I'm the one who is supposed to be nauseous," says my sister, flipping an omelet like a French chef onto her glass plate.

"I know, don't you have morning sickness or something?"

167

"No, not really. But I have been eating a lot of junk food. Pizza. Chips. Yodels. Things I never used to eat."

"Oh don't talk about food, I think I'm going to be sick."

"Maybe you should cut back on the margaritas."

"You know if I'm an alcoholic, Gregor's going to have to pay for rehab—this is all his fault."

WHILE MY SISTER goes out to the gym, I stay at the house, pleading a headache. Lawrence is at work so I am alone. I go outside but the sun hurts my eyes. I go back to the kitchen and fix myself an espresso with Lawrence's fancy Krups machine. I sink into one of their puffy couches and flick on the TV. It's noon and, without thinking, I turn to *All My Children*. Once I start watching, I can't stop. I want to see Gregor. When his character finally appears, at the end of the show, I try to decipher how he's feeling about me. He looks a little distracted, but maybe that's just his character trying to act mysterious. His character, Lord Haines, is on the phone with Switzerland conducting secret business deals. It turns out he is smuggling forged Monets and trying to pass them off to the Pine Valley Museum. The creep.

MY SISTER COMES back from the gym and tells me she knows just the thing for my hangover. "It's a surprise," she says and she won't tell me where we're going.

I sleep in the car and wake up at Palm Tree Spa.

"I can't afford this," I tell her.

"You can pay me back later. Anyway, they're having a special for members of my gym."

My sister and I get the special spa package—a mud bath, herbal wrap and minimassage.

I LOVE THE mud bath, lying in the clean thick warm mud, a cool white towel on my forehead. The mud is clean smelling, and it has a weird buoyancy. They keep piling more mud on top of me as I drift up to the surface. I keep thinking about Gregor nostalgically, as if the mud has totally obliterated his existence. But when I am getting my massage, hot tears stream down my face.

When the massage lady notices, she doesn't seem put out. In fact she seems pleased, as if she's doing a good job. "Massage brings up emotions for a lot of people."

I don't argue and she hands me an aromatherapy tissue. "Just go with the feelings."

She digs with some hard part of her hand into my back until I moan.

AFTERWARD MY SISTER and I have a late lunch at a nearby restaurant that is filled with plants. After the first glass of California chardonnay hits my ultra-relaxed nervous system, I feel giddy.

"That was great, wasn't it," I mumble, trying not to collapse into my Caesar salad.

My sister seems moody, picking at her Greek salad. "Lawrence and I came out here on our first weekend. It was wonderful. I think that's when I got pregnant."

"Why haven't you guys come back? It's very romantic."

"Lawrence is so busy. Proving himself at Splash. I just wish—" My sister starts to say something but then stops herself. "Did I tell you he's doing a pool for Heather Locklear?" The way she changes the subject when it gets uncomfortable reminds me of my mother.

"I love Heather Locklear. *Melrose Place* is a classic."

"It's going to be in the shape of some tattoo she has. A flower I think."

"How original!"

"Lawrence is very creative, although he is constrained by his clients' taste."

I want to say lack of taste, but I stop myself.

Although my sister and I are getting close again, there are certain oblique areas in our relationships, no-man's-lands where I don't dare venture. Like any criticism of Lawrence. Her whole world revolves around him, inside their egg.

"So are you guys getting married?" I ask.

"Yes, Lawrence wants to. As soon as possible. Not because of the baby. He wanted to before. Practically since our first date."

"I'm not surprised. Where?"

"Probably at the parents', in Woodstock, on the lawn."

I have a vision of huge platters of hummus and baba ganoush and my mother in some flowing caftan. I say, "You're kidding," before I can stop myself.

My sister looks offended. "Well, we both like it up there and it's convenient for both our families."

When she says families, I don't feel included.

"Well, the parents will be thrilled. First the baby and now this. Lawrence isn't going to make you become a house-wife, is he?"

My sister just shakes her head at me in disgust.

WE GET IN the habit of watching *All My Children* every day, just like we did in high school. If we go out, I set it up to tape.

"This is sick, Liza. I don't think you should be watching this," says my sister, but I can tell she's getting into the plot of the show.

Today, we watch the whole show, but Gregor doesn't appear. I feel upset.

"Do you think they've cut out his character? What about

the art gallery opening?" I ask my sister. "Do you think he'll be there? This is the gala event of the year in Pine Valley."

"I thought you hated him."

"I do. I'm curious." I pause, and turn off the TV with the remote. "You're right, I shouldn't watch this. I have to go on with my life. Bette, remember you said Lawrence might know of a job, could you ask him?"

*L*ATER, WHEN LAWRENCE gets home, we all have a cocktail together, sitting on their puffy white couches. Lawrence and I have martinis in huge V-shaped glasses and my sister has cranberry juice and soda.

She looks at our drinks with envy.

I say, "I bet our mother drank through all her pregnancies."

"Yeah, she probably smoked too," says Bette, sipping her cranberry juice, "but I don't want the guilt."

Lawrence turns to me. He is wearing a Mickey Mouse T-shirt and looks like he has always lived in California. "So, Liza, I think I might have a job for you."

"Really, what?"

"Well this guy I know has a small production company and they're always hiring people to read scripts. I told him you'd be perfect. It doesn't pay much but—"

"That's okay," I interrupt, "I wasn't making much walking dogs."

"Are you still getting unemployment?" asks Bette.

"I thought it was over, but I actually have two months left. It's so weird, you can call in from here."

"I set up an interview for you. Tomorrow at ten-thirty."

"Tomorrow?!"

"Don't worry, it's casual. And you should bring a writing sample."

171

Liza the Lemming stayed in Fire Island for a few days. She slept on the beach, although the nice boys she met offered her a place at their pink oceanfront beach house. Unfortunately, they had a large territorial dog who expressed his dislike of Liza with a growl that said, "Get the hell out of here you little runt," and she was not interested in tangling with him again.

During the day, while the big nasty dog was out on the beach interrupting beach volleyball games and kicking sand in people's lunches, Liza wandered around the house, reading books, books she had never seen before. Human books. The lemming translations missed a lot she realized. She especially liked the children's books, Winnie the Pooh, Wind on the Willows, The Phantom Tollbooth. She saw a human encyclopedia lying on the coffee table and read items at random, turning over the heavy pages with some difficulty. Arctic, ostrich, turnip. Sure that her people were not mentioned in the book, she looked under "l" for "lemming." Liza was pleasantly surprised to come across a listing for lemmings. In fact there was a picture of a very unattractive lemming, of the genus Swedish Leminus, which all the other lemmings despised, staring out at her. Nevertheless, seeing one of her fellow creatures, she felt homesick.

Lemming
A mouselike rodent of arctic or northern regions, inhabiting tundra or open meadows. All are about 5 in. (13 cm) long, with stout bodies, thick fur, and short tails.

She read on further.

When the population of the lemmings gets too dense, they engage in a ritual migration, which often ends in their drowning in deep waters.

172

Liza the Lemming felt all her fur standing up on end. She thought about the wilderness training, the migration. Only the strongest would survive, like they were taught in ecobiology. The strongest would survive and make new lemming colonies, and the others, her friends, even Sandor, and all the little lemlets, well she couldn't even bear to think about it. It was all becoming frighteningly clear.

She walked outside, feeling chilled, even in the hot sun. And all of a sudden, looking out at the blue, blue water, she knew in the bottom of her soul what she had to do.

She had to save them.

Chapter Seventeen

I DON'T KNOW what to wear to the interview. It's fall but in LA it feels more like summer. All my clothes are black. Everyone out here dresses in light colors: white, pale green, shocking pink. I feel like a black crow flying over all the pastel birds.

I WAIT IN a glossy foyer of the office of a man named Ivan Bearman, Lawrence's friend. He works at a production company called Excess. The office is like a fun house, with glass and mirrors everywhere. I clasp my manila folder with my Liza the Reluctant Lemming story. My writing sample. I showed it to Bette and Lawrence and they said it was cute, but maybe a little self-indulgent. Lawrence actually said it and Bette agreed, because there can't be any disagreement in their world. It was the first time Lawrence ever reminded me of Tad.

I FIND THEIR constant agreement strange because when we were little, there were always disagreements. Not loud, but painful. My parents had "discussions" that were like strategic military events. They never fought, they discussed, they talked. If I did something unacceptable, my father would have a "talk" with me. The most vivid discussion between my parents is the one they had about Judaism. My mother argued that Judaism was a nationality and my father's position was that it was a religion. Now, it seems like a relatively harmless topic but my parents debated for weeks, until their "discussions" disintegrated into nasty comments and finally a long silence.

WHEN THE MAN I assume is Ivan Bearman comes out, after I have waited for forty-three minutes in his refrigerator of an office, he walks out to the waiting room and right past me. He is a balding man in jeans and a thick white turtleneck and it's obvious he has no idea who I am. I know this is a moment that calls for assertive action, but I just watch him walk by and into the door labeled M.

As he is on his way back, I gather up my courage and my manila folder and stand up. He stops and looks at me, a dark blot on the reflective surface of his waiting room.

"You are Mr. Bearman?" He looks at me, puzzled, but not unfriendly.

"Liza, Liza Ferber," I say.

"And you are?" I can see his brain clicking under his balding head.

I let him dangle in uncertainty for a moment, considering the possibility that I might be someone important.

"I was sent by Lawrence Northrup," I say, slowly, pausing between each word. "Splash. Script reading. Interview."

"Right, right, well I guess you can come in," he says, as if relinquishing a point in a debate.

I walk into his office, a lacquered nightmare, framed by a

huge window dominating one wall. I am magnetically drawn toward the window and stand there in front of the invisible glass sure that I will fall right through and forty-two floors down onto what looks like a huge parking lot.

I say, "Great window."

He stands by the window and I steel myself to stand nearby, fighting waves of vertigo.

He stares out the window as if searching for something and I thrust my manila envelope toward him.

"My writing sample," I say decisively.

He takes the folder and a few moments later, says, "Good."

I feel as if we are having a conversation out of synch, a long-distance phone call in two separate languages.

He tells me about all the exciting projects his studio is doing. "We've got some great pilots in the works. Very funny stuff."

I remember my father telling me that the key to an interview is to imitate the interviewer's body posture. Ivan crosses his arms and leans forward. I cross my arms and lean forward.

"That's great."

While I am plunging downward in the elevator, I realize he never said a word about the actual job.

BACK AT THE house, over grilled chicken (Lawrence loves to grill), Bette and Lawrence hover and ask me how it went. I feel like a child having brought home an inferior report card.

"Great," I say, wanting it to be true. "He seemed really interested. He said he'd get back to me."

"Hmm," says Lawrence, flipping the chicken breasts over.

"Did he look at your story?" asks Bette, frowning.

"Well, not right then, but he said he'd get it to the right people, and someone would get back to me."

"Well, I hate to burst your bubble, Liza, but that sounds like a rejection." Lawrence waves his fork at me.

"Lawrence, stop being so negative," says Bette.

LAWRENCE TELLS ME over dinner, "I've got a job for you Liza. It's not glamorous but you'll be outside and you'll get paid in cash."

AFTER DINNER, THE phone rings. "You know that could be him now," I say, halfheartedly.

My sister hands the phone to me. "It's mom."

I get on the phone and my mother says, "Liza, are you okay? I just talked to Gregor and he is very worried about you."

"Mom, this is between me and him, please . . ."

"How are you going to work this out if you refuse to speak to him?"

"Mom, do you know what he did??"

"All I know is that relationships are a lot of work. You know your father and I have had our problems too. Things happen."

"Mom, I don't want to talk about this with you."

"Liza, listen, there's something I want to tell you."

"Mom . . ."

"There's something that happened to me that I think could help you."

"What are you talking about?"

"Remember when I had to go to Sweden? I was finishing my dissertation at the Institute."

I have a vague memory of my father cooking lots of hamburgers and speaking to my mother on the phone. "Yeah, I remember."

"Well, something happened over there, between me and a colleague."

"You had an affair?"

"Well, I don't know if I would characterize it as an affair, but yes, I did have an involvement. Your father and I were having problems and—"

"Oh, my God. I can't believe this. Who was he?"

"It's not important."

"Not that weird guy with the beard, Sven, was it?"

"It doesn't matter who it was, my point is that your father and I worked it out."

"Dad knows about it?"

"Liza, this happened twenty years ago."

"And Daddy knew about it?"

"Yes, it was difficult but we actually became a lot closer afterward."

"Mom, this is really weird. I think I may have to get off the phone. You're not still seeing Sven, are you?"

"Liza, don't be ridiculous. My point is that you have to talk to Gregor. Do you want me to talk to him for you?"

"Mom, promise me, you won't talk to Gregor. Whatever you do, do not call him."

I RUSH TO the phone each time it rings, but after my mother, no one calls for me. I can't seem to digest what my mother told me but all of a sudden, it seems crucial I get this job, to prove that I can do something, not just be a girlfriend, or scatterbrained Liza who still doesn't know what she's doing with her life. I want to tell people, "I read scripts, at Excess."

THE STUDIO DOESN'T call. Gregor doesn't call. I get a letter from him. I don't know if I've ever gotten a letter from him before. I got postcards when he was in summer stock, but never

179

a letter. He says he's sorry. For what happened, and that he hurt me and that he loves me . . . very much. That he isn't going to bother me anymore but will wait until I get in touch with him. I feel myself softening as I read the letter so I stuff it down the garbage disposal until it disappears in a flurry of white specks. I am not going to sink back into that. My mother had an affair. I have to get this job.

I CALL UP the studio and ask to speak to Mr. Bearman. "This is Liza, Liza Ferber, I came in for an interview the other day."

"Mr. Bearman is on a conference call, can I have him get back to you?"

"Mr. Bearman is in a script meeting, can I take a message?"

"Mr. Bearman is unavailable."

I TELL MY sister over *All My Children*, "Okay it doesn't look good, but I still think there's hope. Maybe he just hasn't had a chance to read—"

"Liza, let's watch."

We haven't watched in a day and Gregor's character seems to have disappeared under mysterious circumstances. The police have been called in by the museum to search for him and several valuable paintings, which have disappeared as well.

"Maybe we should call the show and find out if Lord Haines is coming back?"

"No," says my sister. "If you want to know, call Gregor."

"Maybe I should take that job Lawrence was talking about."

OUT IN THE blazing sun, I rake leaves across the surface of a pool. Me, college graduate, daughter of two college professors with doctorates, cleaning pools. I trip over my rake, scraping my knee against the nubby surface of the cement.

I LIE IN bed, looking up at the ceiling. I am exhausted from cleaning pools. My body aches in every joint. My hands are raw. Cleaning pools. I wonder if it would make any difference if I was in some profession that I approved of: shrink, writer, artist, college professor. What if none of those things would make me happy? If living with Gregor didn't make me happy, why would a profession? Maybe I was happy, I just didn't realize it. This idea of happiness is like a puzzle I can't fit together, one shiny jagged piece just out of my reach.

I think of my mother, in Sweden, with Sven. All I can think of are pieces of Ingmar Bergman movies I've seen, with dark cold interiors and women with tortured faces. I see my mother walking in the snow with big fuzzy boots, telling Sven that she must go back.

"But what about the Dream Institute?" he asks, "What about our passion?"

"It is not meant to be, Sven."

I drift off to sleep, tossing and turning.

MAYBE IT'S THE maternal hormones surging through her system, but my sister is constantly baking. Tortes and pies and complicated dinners with strange ingredients. As far as the pregnancy, there are no visible signs. She remains thin, without morning sickness, although she can't bear the smell of coffee.

As a rule, Lawrence comes home late, and I leave them alone for candlelit dinners of poached salmon and fennel or jerk chicken or thai hot pot. Lawrence is always touching Bette, holding her hand, stroking her back, and it makes me uncomfortable. Since she's been pregnant, he's taken to stroking her flat stomach in front of me. I've taken to eating cheese toast in the kitchen and then drifting upstairs, to watch TV or read. I've been reading science fiction books, books that transport me to alien worlds, intergalactic battles, fights against avatars in cyberspace.

TONIGHT, MY SISTER is making her strange foods for a dinner party, for the couple who live next door. I know from Bette's phone messages that she has become friendly with the woman, Miranda. They both are actors.

I try to like them but fail. Miranda flounces in wearing a lime green, vinyl pantsuit and doesn't shut up until she's out the door again. On first glance, she seems attractive, but as the evening wears on, her features appear coarser and coarser. She talked about her agent, her manager, this great part she's going to get. Lawrence and Bette hang on her every word.

We drink martinis. Miranda seems surprised I haven't heard of her. Apparently, she has had minuscule parts on some of the worst television shows around.

She tells us over dinner that she has developed a new attitude toward her success: Now she knows it will happen; it's just a question of when.

"There's a lot of jealousy in this business," she tells us all, as if the powers that be have sabotaged her career because of her excess of talent. "But I know I have the talent, and the looks, and the commitment."

Bette and Lawrence nod in agreement.

BEN, MIRANDA'S HUSBAND, is dark and moody, but at least he attempts to talk to me. After a few minutes, however, when he realizes that I'm not in the business and won't be able to help him in his dark and moody path toward stardom, he lights up a Camel and slinks back over to his wife.

After they leave, Lawrence goes to his study to do some work and I help my sister clean up.

I LOVE THE feel of the soapy hot water on my hands, and the quiet after everyone has left.

"You didn't like them, did you?" says Bette.

"Do you want me to be honest?"

"Of course."

"Miranda seems incredibly self-absorbed. I mean that whole speech about her inevitable success, I mean, please . . . and she ignored me the whole evening."

My sister gestures with a snowy white dishcloth. "You just don't understand. Miranda had a really difficult childhood. That confidence, it's just her persona."

I think of Gregor, rehearsing his scenes, how he would become the part he was auditioning for, the time he grew a beard to try out for *Three Sisters*, its roughness against my face.

"It's not like I haven't been around actors."

"I know, but LA's different. Anyway, Miranda's been really helpful to me. When I first got here, Lawrence was working really hard and she took me shopping, introduced me to people. She really took me under her wing."

I picture the dark scraggly wing of a vulture.

MY SISTER'S ABILITY to deceive herself amazes me. First she deceived herself about her ex-husband, Tom, that they were so blissfully happy. Afterward, she told me that it hadn't been good for a while. Then after they broke up, she deceived herself that she was blissfully happy being alone, that she didn't need anyone. And now, she's blissfully happy with Lawrence, and loves LA and all these superficial people and doesn't need anything but cooking and having a baby. Maybe this self-deception is genetic because I've obviously deceived myself about Gregor. Not to mention my mother. I thought that things were going so well with us. And I thought my parents had the perfect marriage. I know I'm avoiding dealing with Gregor, but I'm not ready to face him. I have to work something out first. And that something has to work out here, far away from him, in LA.

THE NEXT MORNING, my sister asks me if I'm working.

"Luckily, I'm off today, which is a good thing because I'm sore all over."

"Lawrence wants me to pick out a birthing center. Do you want to go with me?"

"A what?"

"A birthing center. You know for the event that's happening in five and a half months."

"I know, I know. Sure, that'd be fun."

WHEN WE WALK into the birth center, I expect to hear screaming. Instead, it's like the reception area at the hairdresser's. They offer us decaf coffee and magazines.

184

"It doesn't seem like a hospital, does it?" I whisper to my sister.

The receptionist, overhearing me, says, "We have one of the lowest rates for cesareans. And in case of any problems, there is an NICU on-site."

"A what?" asks my sister anxiously.

"A neonatal intensive care unit."

I look around as we are escorted to the sales office. The center is furnished like a hotel for old ladies, lots of flowery patterns over everything, dainty chairs, swoopy curtains in dark pink.

We wander through the rooms, and a representative named Mandy comes over and points out the features of the room.

"We're very mother-friendly here, as well as baby-friendly. This is our LDRP, a labor, delivery, recovery, postpartum room. You never have to leave. There's the whirlpool bath, to ease the pain," she says confidentially, "during labor." She seems to be speaking to me as if I am the expectant one and my sister does nothing to dispel this notion.

"Right, right," I say, hurrying out of the claustrophobic room. I feel that I am being sold an efficiency apartment, a studio where I can cook, sleep, and entertain all in one room.

"We have traditional birthing assistants, doulas. We also have birthing support groups. Oh, and this is a great feature, a patient-controlled analgesic machine, so you can control your own pain medication.

My sister is looking green, as if she has never connected the fact that she is pregnant with the fact that she is going to have to give birth.

"I'M GOING TO make tea," I tell my sister when we get home. "Earl Grey, with lots of milk and sugar."

My sister seems in a daze. "Do you know that birth is never really mentioned in Victorian literature?"

"I've noticed that."

"I've had nothing to prepare me. It's so overwhelming."

"I know you'll be a great mother. You helped me when I was little. Remember when I used to barricade myself in my room, and wait for someone to come get me and no one did . . . except you?"

"Yes, but what about all those times I baby-sat for you and Danny and ignored you?"

My sister is sniffling now and I hand her a tissue.

"Look, it's probably the hormones. That's why you're upset."

"I want this baby, I really do, it's only that Lawrence thinks I'm some sort of maternal expert because I'm a woman and I know nothing about it. I expect it to come out in swaddling clothes with a nanny."

"Well, I'm sure he could arrange that," I almost tease.

"And he assumes I'll want to stay home forever . . ."

"What do you want?"

"I don't know. I really miss the university. My cubicle at the library."

"You have to talk to him, Bette."

"I know."

Chapter eighteen

ALL I WANT is to forget about Gregor, but when I wake up he is this weight pressing against my chest. At least I'm not in New York anymore. The one thing I learned from my breakup with Charles was that staying in the same city as your ex prolongs the pain. Of course it didn't help that I used to go to every place Charles and I went together, the Fog City Diner, the café we liked, that place out at the beach where you could watch the sea lions. I tracked all our happy moments, as if I were conducting a tour of our relationship. But Gregor is not Charles and I can't start thinking about all the things I miss about him or I'll be lost.

I DON'T TALK to my sister about all this, because she's always with her new friend Miranda. They go shopping, the gym.

"You're welcome to come along," Bette tells me, as if I'm going to enjoy watching them exercise their charge cards and discuss Miranda's imminent stardom.

This unlikely friendship between my sister and Miranda is the first event that has forged a small silent bond between me and Lawrence. Lawrence claims to like Miranda but I believe he is beginning to tire of her chunky gold jewelry and ridiculous pronouncements on life.

"Everyone over forty needs a face-lift," she told me once while she was waiting for Bette to get herself ready for a trip to Miranda's gym. Miranda takes her everywhere, like a pet. Despite being pregnant, Bette seems to like the constant activity.

Lawrence doesn't say anything but looks tired when Bette talks about Miranda.

I think Lawrence would prefer Bette to stay in and knit little baby things with tassels but Bette doesn't even seem to remember that she's pregnant most of the time. Miranda takes her everywhere, to her Rolfer, her hairdresser, her personal shopper. In return, Bette gives Miranda reading lists and script advice. Miranda credits my sister for helping her land a part in a tour of the musical *Landlord*. It's about all these hippies who become traders and buy apartment buildings in the East Village. Miranda plays an evil landlord named Evicta. I think it's perfect casting.

My sister is developing that slightly brittle LA look, the look of someone who is extensively groomed and shod but hasn't had quite enough to eat.

I T'S MONDAY MORNING and I put on my green overalls and go downstairs for some food. It's a sunny day in October and I'm going to my pool-cleaning job. I like the anonymity of this job. Generally there's no one home at the houses I service, so after I've finished raking and checking the filters, I doze on lounge chairs until the truck appears.

"More frittata darling?" Bette calls out from the kitchen to Lawrence who is in the dining room reading *Variety*. Lately,

Bette's been experiencing morning sickness, so now she only eats crackers in the mornings, but she still makes elaborate meals for Lawrence as if she's making up for something. I eat what I want: toast dripping with butter.

Lawrence stands up and wipes nonexistent crumbs from his khaki suit. "Thanks, no, I've got to run. What are you girls up to today?"

"Miranda and I are going to this amazing photography exhibit at the LA County Museum."

"The one of the woman who takes naked pictures of her children?" I ask.

My sister nods.

"Freud would have a field day."

"Miranda says it's fabulous. Not prurient at all."

"I'm sure Miranda doesn't know what prurient is," I say.

Lawrence gives me a wink on his way out the door.

"Well have a good time, don't tire yourself out." He kisses Bette lightly and leaves.

"So Liza, you want to come to this exhibit with us?" asks Bette, applying lipstick.

"No, I have two pools today, one new, in West Hollywood. Otherwise I'd love to."

PICKING UP LEAVES around the enormous-eggplant shaped pool, I recite a list of the things I like about my job to myself, like a mantra: Fresh air. Alone. Independent. Fresh air. Alone. Independent. If I save my money I will soon be able to afford a little place of my own. I will get a cat and name it Boris. I'll learn to drive. I clean out the hose from the underwater vacuum, humming the theme from the *Mary Tyler Moore Show*.

A food stylist named Klaus owns this pool. Not only is the pool in the shape of an eggplant, but the chairs look like various vegetables I can't stand. Sitting in a zucchini, I scribble on my notepad ideas for my Liza the Lemming stories. She is in

Paris now, living in a hotel, resting after her ordeal. She wants to meet Catherine Deneuve. I reread the part where she tries to save the lemmings.

Liza the Lemming's cab sped down to the beach. She would have been here earlier, but her flight to California was delayed and the airline had tried to put her in the baggage compartment. After a heated discussion with the airline manager, she ended up flying in first class and drinking beer out of a real glass. As Liza neared the cliff, she saw that the lemmings were already jumping, their sleek dark forms crashing headfirst into the water.

"Stop!!" Liza called out, leaping out of the cab. "It's too deep, you'll drown." She couldn't make out who had jumped, but she thought she saw Sandor's red backpack sinking into the stormy water.

She yelled until her lungs were raw, but they were too far away to hear her. She couldn't even make out the shapes of the lemmings anymore, just the water, foaming and hostile. I should have called the coast guard, she thought, the national guard, the police. Someone. What was I thinking? She put her tiny paws up to her eyes and cried.

Just then, glancing down, she saw a tiny parachute open, then another, then another, until the water was dotted with little white specs. The specs were moving across the water with a whirring sound. The lemmings were being carried by these motorized parachutes. They must have had them in their backpacks. They were migrating, like it said in the encyclopedia, but they weren't going to die. They were going to make it!

After cleaning the second pool, I am lulled into a meditative state. I like this small pool, it's not pretentious, not designed by Lawrence or anyone else from Splash. It's old, with slightly crumbling Spanish tiles and moss drooping down onto the shallow end. I imagine an aging B-movie actress living here, with platinum hair and high-heeled mules. It's the kind of pool that owners generally clean themselves but, according to my sheet, they have me scheduled to come here every day this week. I have to remind myself to bring a book tomorrow.

WHEN I GET back to the house, my sister is on her way out again.

"How was the photography show?" I ask. She gives me a postcard of two androgynous children playing in a waterfall.

"Interesting," I say noncommittally. "Where are you going now?"

"Power yoga."

"Isn't that a contradiction in terms? Aren't you supposed to go to Lamaze class?"

My sister is out the door and I don't know if she heard me. "Oh, Liza you got a phone call."

"Gregor?"

"No, some guy, very mysterious, said he'd call back."

THE SECOND DAY at the new pool, I am deep into my new book about a group of alienated future psychics who escape six million years back through time, into the Pliocene epoch, only to be overtaken by evil aliens. The sun is warm on my overalls, and I drift off, dreaming about prehistoric animals and time travel. A faint noise enters my consciousness, and a dark shape blots out the sun.

I blink up at a comforting familiar face. It's Gregor. I reach up to him, still half asleep, twining my hands around his neck, pulling him down to me like coming home. He kisses me and I

191

wake up and it is Gregor. I push him away from me as hard as I can.

He falls into the water with a loud splash.

"What are you doing here, you're supposed to be in New York!!!" I yell in after him.

Gregor sloshes up the crumbly steps of the pool. He is dripping from his white shirt all the way down to his leather moccasins.

I shake my head. "I can't believe you're the one renting this house. Who told you where I was working? How did you find me? It was my mother, wasn't it? I can't believe her."

Gregor takes off his shoes and empties them into the pool, "You wouldn't talk to me Liza. What was I supposed to do?"

"Are you out here for an audition?"

"No. I came to see you. You haven't been the easiest person to get hold of. Did you get my messages?"

"No one asked you to come here. Look, I've got to get back to work."

I yank the vacuum roughly out of the water and put it away, practically tangling myself up in the process. I don't look at Gregor but I can feel him staring at me.

He walks toward me. "Liza, stop this!"

"Don't come any closer," I warn him. "Look, I'm not the one who . . ."

Gregor comes even closer.

"Stay there."

"Liza, I want to explain."

"There is nothing to explain. You're a free agent. Isn't that what you always said, that's what you're always saying, that you could be gone at any moment. Well, now you have your wish."

A loud honk punctuates the silence.

"That's my ride, I've got to go."

I'VE ALWAYS THOUGHT I want to know the details of everything, that only by knowing all the details would I be able to understand the meaning, but right now I don't want to know anything. I just want to get away from Gregor. Alone. Outdoors. Independent.

THE REST OF the day goes by in a blur of chlorine and leaves. But Gregor's here, a little voice inside my head whispers. What do I do about this information?

WHEN I GET back to the house, it's quiet. I take a hot bubble bath and try to think about Gregor being here. What will happen. I don't have to go back there. I don't have to ever see him again. I think about the stunned expression on his face when I pushed him into the pool and I pour in more bubbles and stretch my legs out in the hot water.

I GO BACK THE next day. I don't tell my sister and Lawrence about Gregor's sudden appearance. I just need to see him one more time before I can be free of him. When the truck gets to the little house, my palms feel clammy. I wipe them quickly on my pants. I think about my father. How could he have forgiven my mother for having an affair? What if he hadn't? I imagine my parents, divorced, arguing about who got to live with whom. I would have probably ended up with my mother. Or maybe we would have all ended up with my father and my mother would have gone away with Sven on a permanent sabbatical. I would have stepbrothers and -sisters with Scandinavian names that sound like sneezes.

I WALK DOWN the narrow path to the pool. I wonder how I look. Maybe Gregor won't even be here. Maybe he's gone back to New York. Given up.

NO. HE'S HERE. And he is sitting at a small table in front of two of those silver domes they use in restaurants to keep food warm. I smell coffee and something delicious.

As if it's in a script, I walk over to the table and sit across from him, not saying a word, and he lifts a cover off one of the domes with a flourish, displaying buttery hot croissants and tiny pots of raspberry jam.

"You must feel really guilty." I look at Gregor. He doesn't look guilty, he looks good, slightly tan in a pair of jeans and a white shirt. I'm glad he's not wearing a bathing suit.

He pours me coffee.

"This is really nice, but it doesn't change anything."

"I know."

I sip my coffee and look at the silver domes. He knows I love things like this, room service, afternoon tea, treats. I decide to try to be civil.

"So, what happened to Lord Haines and *All My Children?*"

"He's dead."

"I know, but what happened?"

"I had them kill me off."

I bite into a warm buttery croissant. Gregor pours me coffee. Puts in milk. One sugar.

"Why?"

"I told you I wanted to see you."

"You mean this"—I wave my hand around to indicate the

194

pool, the house, the breakfast—"this isn't for some audition? You really came out to see me?"

"Yes. I'm groveling, Liza."

I smile for the first time, and at the same time, start crying. I get up almost before I realize I am moving. "I have to go." I say this knowing my ride won't come for at least another hour.

"But you haven't finished your croissant."

"See what you've driven me to? I'm going to wait out front for my ride. I want to be alone, okay?"

I SIT ON THE stone wall outside the house and think about Gregor. I imagine him touching someone else.

I walk back to the pool. "Why?"

Gregor looks puzzled.

"Why did you do it?"

He takes a deep breath as if he's been waiting for this. "I don't know, I guess it was getting the part in the soap. It made me feel invulnerable, that I could do anything and get away with it. And to be honest I guess she flattered me."

"And I suppose you didn't think it wouldn't hurt your career."

"No."

Gregor sits closer, touching my arm.

I pull it away. "Don't."

"It was stupid, I realized it right away."

"During or after?"

"Liza don't do this."

195

IT TAKES ALL my strength not to cry in the truck in front of all the other pool guys.

"Are you okay?" a guy named Sean asks me.

"Allergies," I say.

BACK AT THE house, I look for my sister, Lawrence, anyone.

The phone rings.

"Gregor?"

"No, Liza?"

"Yes. Who is this?"

"This is Claude from Excess."

"About the job for Mr. Bearman?" Finally, I think.

"Job? No, this is about your script."

"My script?" What is he talking about?

"Yes, I'm part of Excess's new creative team and we all love your script. We'd like to produce it."

"Uh-huh." I find it hard to focus on what he's saying.

"We need you to come down and discuss the details."

"Are you sure you have the right person?"

"You wrote *Liza the Reluctant Lemming*, right? It's great, going to make a great cartoon."

"Cartoon?"

"Yes. Why don't you come down tomorrow around eleven."

Chapter
nineteen

I GET READY TO go to the meeting at the studio for *Liza the Reluctant Lemming*. I want to tell my sister about it, but I want to wait until I know it's really happening. I haven't told her about seeing Gregor either. I'm not sure why. It's weird having this whole secret life she knows nothing about.

In the mirror, I notice the dyed part of my hair has totally grown out to its natural brown. I pin my hair back with tiny rhinestone clips, try to decide on a look for the meeting. I need to look like an artist who means business. I put on mascara and lipstick in bold, creative strokes.

I run downstairs to catch Bette before she leaves for whatever Miranda has planned for her day. "Hey Bette, can I borrow your white blazer?"

"Sure, where are you going?"

"I've got a kind of an interview."

"Really?"

I turn back up the stairs. "Look, I'll tell you all about it later. Are you going to be around? Let's go out for dinner."

"Dinner?" my sister says, as if it's a new concept. "Sure. Why not."

"Around seven."

"Okay, I'll see you later."

"If this works out, it'll be my treat."

AT THE STUDIO, I am whisked into a large conference room. The whole look of Mr. Bearman's office has been changed and he is conspicuously absent. Instead of hi-tech modern, there's a Southwestern theme, with Navajo rugs and hangings and colors like a desert. I am introduced to four people and we sit around a low coffee table etched with native designs. Everyone is drinking herbal teas so I have some too.

I sip my tea.

"So what happened to Mr. Bearman?" I ask to no one in particular.

"Downsized."

"Outsourced."

"Redundant."

"He didn't fit in with the new concept of the studio."

Brad, a hyper guy in his twenties who seems to be running the meeting, says earnestly, "Now Liza, we want your input on everything."

"Great cartoon."

"Loved it."

"Well, I didn't write it as a cartoon. It was a children's story," I say.

"With just a few minor changes it's going to be perfect," says a thin man at the head of the table.

"Action cartoons for boys are getting very good demographics in the male ten-to-twelves," says a blonde at the other end. "How would you feel about having Liza be a boy?"

"Not good. I would feel not good about it."

"I see her more as a Pocahontas, saving the poor lemmings in a sexy outfit."

"She's not Pocahontas either. And she's not even a teenager."

"Right. Of course."

"Well, the first thing we have to do is figure out a look for the show," says a woman named Daphne who introduced herself to me as the concept editor. "The colors, I see purple, lots of purple."

"Liza, I want to run something by you, we have a great idea for the voice, that comedian with the low voice, you know, Janeane Garofalo, the comic. Do you remember that movie she did a couple of years ago with Uma Thurman?"

"She has a great stand-up routine."

"Uma Thurman's amazing-looking," says Daphne.

Finally something I can agree with. "Oh I like her. Janeane Garofalo, not Uma Thurman."

I COME HOME from the meeting dazed. They said a lot of things but I can't seem to remember much of it. I have a number of business cards in my pocketbook, cards with telephone numbers, voice mail numbers, fax numbers, pager numbers, service numbers, e-mail numbers and URLs. I can reach anyone at any time. They're going to fax me storyboards. I want to start writing the next segment of the story anyway. I told them about Liza in Paris and they loved it. I'm not clear what they're going to pay me for this either. I said I was going to have to talk to my lawyer and they looked very impressed and started throwing out terms like *percentage points* and *subrights*. I'll have to call Tad; maybe he can help me with the contracts. He is

Lawrence's brother, after all, my future semirelative, my brother-in-law in-law.

I WANDER AROUND my sister's house aimlessly. Her house is pale white and beautiful but I miss Gregor and my sooty New York apartment, our crumbling New York walls, even the roar of the garbage trucks in the morning. I feel insubstantial here in California. California itself is insubstantial, about to be swallowed back into the earth or swept out to the ocean.

I take books out of the bookcase, books my sister used to study so carefully for her dissertation, books that look out of place in this glossy room. I pull out a Barbara Pym novel and start reading, sinking cross-legged into the plush white carpeting. It's about a woman who, after a breakup, moves into a little cottage on the outskirts of a small village, and her encounters with the shy local clergyman and nosy villagers.

I TRY TO read but the words swim like small fish. They want to make my story into a cartoon. My Story. I hug this knowledge to me like a tiny Belgian chocolate that I have saved to eat in a private moment. Liza the Lemming will exist. Maybe Bette's Jane will even see my cartoon on TV someday.

This is probably the most exciting thing that has ever happened to me and I know I should be happy but I keep thinking of the white shirt Gregor was wearing when I saw him yesterday. It's one of those soft white cotton shirts he always wears. He never wears short-sleeved shirts, not even here in LA, where it is eighty-five degrees. My analyst used to say that the most important thing I could do was to feel all my feelings. I thought this was ridiculous. How could you not feel all your feelings? But now I have so many conflicting emotions I am afraid to feel them all. I am still angry at Gregor, and there is a part of me that wants to stay angry at him forever, just have this one emotion, clear and simple. He betrayed me. He cannot be forgiven.

But things aren't that simple. There's always going to be things I want to tell Gregor. Right now, I want to see him, tell him about Liza the Lemming.

Picking up the portable phone, I punch out the number at the house he's renting, reading it off my work sheet.

When he answers the phone, I don't say anything for a second.

"Liza, is that you?"

"Yes. I—" I hear a faint click in my ear, and I realize it's the call waiting.

"Gregor, I'm sorry, hold on a sec."

I push the button down to get the other line and hear nothing. Stupid portables. I long for a clunky old phone you can't get disconnected from.

"Hello, hello?"

"Liza?"

WHEN I HEAR my sister's voice on the phone, I have the sensation of total quiet, as if everything has stopped, "Bette, what is it?"

"Liza, we had a big fight."

"You and Lawrence?"

"At that restaurant, Hula. When I got home, I started bleeding."

"Are you okay? How's the baby? Where are you?"

"St. Judes, Room 207. They don't know yet."

"I'll be right there."

I PRAY IN THE cab, pray for my sister, the baby, please let them be OK, please.

The hospital is so much nicer than the one my mother stayed in that it seems impossible for anything bad to happen in it.

My sister is lying in a bed, pale and thin. "Are you okay?" I ask her.

"It's all my fault, Liza."

"Don't be ridiculous."

I take my sister's hand. It is very cold.

"I told him I didn't know how I felt about the baby."

"Where is he?"

"He left. He said he needed to think. And now look what happened."

"It's going to be okay. Lawrence loves you. You had a fight. If he knew about this, he'd be here. Do you want me to beep him?"

My sister shakes her head. "No, I can't talk to him, not till I know. Don't call him."

The doctor comes in to examine my sister. I wait out in the hall.

I SEE MIRANDA at the bottled water dispenser and for a second I feel almost glad to see someone familiar. She actually looks concerned.

We confer about Bette in hushed tones.

"She looks so sick, we have to call Lawrence," She says, biting a French-manicured nail.

"No, we have to do what Bette wants."

"But he should know."

"No!" I am firm. I change the subject. "What happened to *Landlord*? I thought you were supposed to be on tour."

"The project wasn't right for me."

"Maybe she shouldn't have done those power yoga classes."

Miranda sounds guilty. "It was only yoga, for God's sake. No one gets hurt from doing yoga."

"She's more fragile than she seems."

Miranda looks nervously at her watch, "Will you look at the time? I've really got to run. Give these to Bette, will you? It'll take her mind off things." She shoves a pile of scripts in my hand.

As soon as she's out of sight, I dump them in a garbage can labeled INFECTIOUS WASTE.

*M*Y SISTER IS released from the hospital later that afternoon. The doctors say it was simple overexertion, that the baby isn't in any danger. But even though everything is going to be OK, they want her to stay off her feet for a few days. The doctor told her she needs to eat more and exercise less.

WHEN WE GET back to the house, there is no sign of Lawrence. Bette seems to expect this. She acts like he's never coming back.

She lies in bed and I try to cheer her up.

I feel like some hearty nanny in an old movie. "You have to eat something."

I bring her up grilled cheese sandwiches with tomato, which congeal at her bedside table.

"Here, have some tea, PG Tips, with milk and sugar, the way you like it."

She takes the tea and pretends to sip it.

"Do you want to talk about this?"

She starts crying, big heaving sobs. "No, I'm . . . I'm afraid that if I do lose the baby, part of me will be relieved."

I hand her a tissue and sit on the bed. "It's okay." Why do people always say things are going to be OK when things are really bad? That's what Gregor always used to say to me, that everything was going to be OK, and now I'm saying it to Bette. I pat her shoulder.

"You're not going to lose the baby. I need Jane to critique my cartoon when she gets old enough."

"What do you mean?"

"Liza the Lemming. A production company is interested in making it into a cartoon, if they haven't changed their minds."

"Oh Lizzy, that's great, but I thought it was going to be a children's book?"

"You haven't called me that since we were little."

My sister smiles.

"I know a cartoon isn't what I had in mind, but it's growing on me. Except they said something about how they're looking at a more adult market for the cartoon. What do you think?"

"Well, Liza, did you really think it was appropriate for children?"

"I don't know, I didn't really think about it. I just wrote it."

I READ MY sister inspirational passages from Barbara Pym. It seems to relax her.

Around dinnertime, I ask her if she's hungry.

She says, "You know what I feel like Liza? A poached egg on toast. Could you make me one?"

"Well, you're really pushing my culinary limits, but I'll try."

"I'll walk you through it."

"You must be feeling better."

AFTER BETTE EATS the poached egg, she asks for a piece of paper and scribbles some notes.

"What are you doing?"

"I think I need a section on breakfast in my dissertation. Isn't it interesting that the reverend only had one egg, but all the other men get two soft-boiled eggs and a rasher of bacon, to keep up their strength? The women have intrinsic strength, but the men are more fragile."

"I think you're on to something. Bette can I ask you something?"

"Sure . . . what?"

"Did you know about Mom and Sven?"

Bette sits up slowly. "I guess I did . . . .There were hang-ups on the phone. Letters with strange postmarks. I think we both must have known at some level."

"I didn't think I knew but when she told me about it, something kind of clicked in my head. . . . But it's so weird to think that Daddy knew and that he forgave her."

"I'm glad he did. Do you know how cold Sweden is in the winter?" My sister smiles and looks almost like her old self.

"Seriously, though, I can't believe she would do it."

Bette just nods.

"Bette, you're not going to like me saying this, but I think you should work it out with Lawrence. Despite the symbiotic nature of your relationship, you two actually seem really happy together."

"But how could he walk out on me . . . now?"

"Look. He's angry. He had this fantasy of your perfect little family, and you didn't let him know that you weren't sure about it."

"I didn't know how I felt."

"Still, whatever negative feelings you had, you didn't share them with him. I don't think your relationship is so fragile that it can't withstand this. . . . God, I sound like Mom. It's a horrifying thought, but maybe she's right occasionally."

"Do you think I'll be a good mother?"

"I think you'll be a wonderful mother. Really. I know what's going to happen. You are going to make up with Lawrence and have Jane and turn into one of the smug happy families that send out a yearly newsletter with a picture of all the kids—no, a collage of pictures and a paragraph about how you've been so busy fixing up the summerhouse and you're not as young as you used to be."

Bette looked horrified. "Liza, if I ever do that, I give you permission to shoot me."

"Okay. I'm calling Lawrence. No arguments. Do you know where he is?"

"He's probably down in Malibu. Splash has a big site down there. They're doing Jennifer Aniston's pool. There's a number in the kitchen."

IT'S BEEN TWO days. Lawrence hasn't come back yet. I left a message at the site, but I didn't say what happened. Bette made me promise not to. She hasn't lost the baby and seems to be feeling much better. She is writing again, furiously.

Sitting outside on the deck, it occurs to me now why I never wanted children. It's as if I believed that by not having a child, I could avoid the whole cycle of birth and death, not be part of it. In TV shows, there is always a birth for every death. I just wanted to halt the equation, as if having a child was some kind of chain letter I wasn't going to respond to.

But my sister is braver than I am, and I want her to have this baby.

Chapter twenty

WHEN LAWRENCE COMES back and sees Bette lying in bed reading Angela Thirkell, there's no question of their splitting up. She tells him that it's all her fault, and he says it's all his fault. They close the door and I can hear soft murmuring from their room. They are back together again, inside the safety of their egg.

When they emerge from their bedroom in the afternoon, I am in the living room trying to read *Sense and Sensibility*. "Guess what?" says Bette.

Before I have time to say anything, she exclaims, "We're getting married."

She and Lawrence stand there looking at me and even though I wanted them to get back together, for a second I have an urge to say, "No, don't do it, it can only end in disaster." I think about what happened to me and Gregor and I feel like Liza the Lemming trying to stop her fellow lemlets from jumping off a cliff. But the lemmings ended up OK, so maybe Lawrence and Bette can survive happiness.

"Liza, you look stunned," says Lawrence.

"Aren't you going to say anything?" asks Bette.

"Congratulations," I say, starting to tear. I get up to kiss them both on the cheek, "I'm just a little surprised."

"So are we. I think we need some champagne," says Lawrence.

"None for me, sweetie," says my sister, pointing at her stomach.

Lawrence gets up and heads toward the kitchen, "Right. Right. I think there's some Pellegrino in the fridge."

LAWRENCE AND BETTE disappear into the kitchen with their arms around each other and I quickly wipe my eyes. I'm always crying lately. I guess it's good. I'm finally expressing my emotions.

They come out and hand me a glass. Lawrence pours in some Perrier-Jouët.

We clink our glasses.

"So, when are you going to do it?"

Bette looks at Lawrence as if to indicate he shouldn't make a big deal of the wedding, given my relationshipless state. "We don't know. Soon."

"We should toast you too, Liza," says Lawrence. "To the cartoon. Tell me all about it."

"I have a meeting next week. They want to know what I think about the look. I've decided to be more forceful about what I want."

"You tell 'em," says my sister.

"So, have you gotten any money yet?" asks Lawrence.

"Well, your brother is dealing with that. For a small fee, of course."

"Don't let him gouge you."

IN THE MORNING, I go over to the little house where Gregor is staying. I sit on the opposite side of the couch from him, holding a pillow in front of me. It's a little blue pillow with WELCOME embroidered on it in bright yellow stitching. So much has happened in the two months since Gregor and I slept together, since all the molecules in our bodies intermingled. Gregor slept with someone else. I found out my mother had slept with someone else. My sister almost miscarried her baby and now she is getting married. I feel a heaviness in my chest, like something pressing against me. It's a familiar feeling, one I had as a little girl. The knowledge that nothing I could do would ever be enough.

"Liza, don't look at me like that."

"Like what?"

"Like you're afraid of me."

Gregor slides slowly over to me and opens his arms.

I shake my head. "I don't know about this."

He enfolds me in his arms. I hug the pillow tighter inside his arms.

He speaks first. "I'm going back to New York. I haven't gotten any work here and they want to bring Lord Haines back on *All My Children*. They haven't explained the details yet, but I'm going to be rising from the dead."

Gregor smiles, but I feel incapable of responding.

"Are you going back right away?"

"Pretty much. Liza, why don't you come with me, back home?"

I see an image of Gregor and the dragon lady producer, embracing on her black leather couch. I sit up, moving back to the other side of the sofa, crossing my arms over the pillow.

"What about what's-her-name?"

"It's not going to happen again."

I stand up, dropping the pillow. "I can't go back to New York now anyway. I have to work on the cartoon. You know, for once, this isn't about you and your career. It's about me."

W HEN I GET back to the house, Lawrence and Bette are checking out wedding information on a bridal Web site.

"Liza, did you know that the train originated in twelfth-century France and that the length indicated the social status of the bride?"

"Are you going to have a train?"

Bette looks at Lawrence and shakes her head. "No, and I may not even be wearing white."

I look over their shoulders at the list of Web sites. "I can't believe there is really a Web site called Itheewed.com."

"They even have special wedding-planning software," says Lawrence.

"Hey, can I be the maid of honor?"

My sister looks up from the laptop. "Liza, we're not having bridesmaids or a maid of honor. It's going to be simple."

"Whatever," I say. "Maybe you should just have the whole wedding on-line—a virtual wedding. That would be simple."

"What we do have to decide is where we're going to have it. What about Malibu, sweetie?" asks Lawrence.

"You know, Mom's going to want to have it at their house," I say.

"We're definitely having it in LA," says Lawrence. "Maybe at one of the pools I designed."

"You'll see," I predict.

*L*ATER, OVER TEA, my sister asks me, "So how did it go, with Gregor?"

She looks so hopeful. I know she wants me to make up with Gregor. That's what I wanted when I went over there but there is this icicle of anger inside me that makes it impossible.

I break a ginger cookie into little pieces. "It was . . . I don't know. He's going back to New York. They're bringing Lord Haines back."

"Didn't he die in that smuggling raid?"

"No one ever really dies in soap operas."

LAWRENCE AND BETTE go out to dinner to celebrate. I wander around the kitchen, nibbling on the English farmhouse cheeses my sister has been buying again lately. Gregor used to say I was like a little mouse, the way I could sniff out any cheese in the house.

I gather up a tray of provisions—cheese, brown bread, a few Calamata olives and some wine. I take everything up to my room and lie in bed, trying to concentrate on a magazine. All the articles are "how to's." "How to Lose 10 Pounds." I know. Stop eating cheese. "How to Deal with a Difficult Boss." I could have used that at the law firm. "How to Feel Sexy." Oh please.

The more I read, the angrier I get. Anger is flowing in waves all through me. I am angry at Gregor. Angry at my mother. Angry that my sister doesn't want me to be her maid of honor. Is this how I'm going to end up, angry and bitter and nibbling on cheese?

I drink half a bottle of chardonnay and fall into a fitful sleep.

It is a hot day in Pamplona. I am on a balcony, leaning over the cobbled street, waiting. What am I waiting for? The street is empty but the balconies are packed with people—voluptuous women in gaudy red dresses, tiny dark children laughing and screaming, old men smoking tiny black cigars. They all start yelling out a word in Spanish that sounds like a cheer. And in the background I start to hear a dull roar, coming closer. What is that noise? What are we waiting for? The noise is getting louder. Men in tight black pants with red cummerbunds appear down on the street. Starched white shirts. One of the men looks so familiar. Oh my god! It's Gregor. Then I hear them. See them. The bulls. Crashing down the road in a cloud of dust and a horrible roaring. Bulls, an endless stream of bulls. The men pirouette out of danger, waving their scarlet capes bravely, but I can't see Gregor anymore.

I run down endless wooden stairs to get to the street, which is empty except for a few torn streamers and bits of red cloth strewn over the cobblestones. It is so dark I am frightened.

There is a coffin in the middle of the street. I run over to it. I open the heavy lid. Inside, Gregor is lying very still in a white suit. Dead. I know because there is a tiny round hole near his heart. I start weeping, lying over his body, crying, "NO. NO. NO."

The pallbearers come. They push me away so they can shut the coffin. "NO," I scream. "You can't leave him in there, he'll be lonely." I take the stuffed animals from Wind in the Willows, Toad and Mole and Rat, and put them in beside him, so he won't be alone, and then they shut the coffin with a loud bang and take him away.

I wake up, hot wet tears on my face.

A WEEK GOES BY in a flurry of bridal magazines and wedding Web sites. Ever since they decided to get married, my sister finally looks pregnant. All her angles, developed in long years of research and running, are being filled in with baby hormones.

I help her write a guest list.

"Miranda?" I ask, pencil poised to slash out her name.

"She means well."

"The road to hell is paved with good intentions."

"Just leave her on."

"Okay. I can't believe how many relatives Lawrence has."

"I know. Luckily, a lot of them live far away."

I'M ALMOST LATE for my meeting at the studio. It's only been a week and a half, but it seems an eternity since I was last there. I wear the same blazer I wore last time. There are only two people at this meeting, a guy and a girl I have never met before. They introduce themselves as the creative team. His name is Robin and his short hair is dyed very bright yellow and looks exactly like a sponge. Her name is Manley. She is wearing a midriff top and has a ring in her navel encircled by a tattoo. It reminds me of an elaborate door knocker. I stare at the storyboards, trying not to look at his sponge or her door knocker.

They are the first people I've met who are actually going to be working on the cartoon. They show me storyboards of *Liza the Reluctant Lemming*, Episode 1. They have definite ideas about how the cartoon should look. I'm surprised how much I like their rendition of Liza.

213

She has a sleek little lemming body and a face like Winona Ryder.

"I like the expression on her face, it's sad but endearing."

"Yeah, that's what we were going for," says Robin.

"What do you think of the hat?" asks Manley.

"I don't think she would wear that. She hates hats, especially baseball caps."

"You talk like she's real," says Robin. "That's cool."

All through the meeting, I keep thinking of Gregor. What if he had died?

"How about the outfit in this one?" asks Manley, pointing to Liza in a bikini.

"I don't know, I think she is more the one-piece type."

"We're trying to gear it toward a more adult audience."

"But it's for children, right?"

"Have you thought about future episodes?" asks Robin, changing the subject.

"I think maybe she'll go to Spain."

THAT AFTERNOON, I watch *All My Children*. Lord Haines enters a room at the museum and Erica practically faints. Seeing Gregor's face, I let out a great deep breath of relief.

Erica pulls herself together and advances toward Gregor/Lord Haines. "Lord Haines. But you're dead!"

The new Lord Haines speaks with a southern accent. "I am terribly sorry to give you such a fright, ma'am. I know I resemble my brother greatly."

He puts out his hand with a flourish. "May I introduce myself, I am Tristan Haines, the black sheep of the family."

Tristan is not really Lord Haines's brother, I learn later in the episode. He is his evil clone.

On soap operas, it's so easy. You do something horrible, you get killed, and then you still get a second chance. Lord Haines the art smuggler was murdered, and Pine Valley thought it was safe from the Art Mafia. But a mad scientist saved a scraping of his skin from a martini glass, and the evil clone Tristan is back stealing masterpieces.

*M*Y PARENTS ARRIVE in LA to help plan Lawrence and Bette's wedding.

"Isn't this wonderful Liza? First the baby, and now the wedding. I was beginning to have my doubts that any of you were going to reproduce."

"Well, some of us are not planning on it."

My parents are ecstatic and ensconced in my room. I have been relegated to the pullout couch in the living room.

"I'm moving out soon anyway," I tell them, trying to fit sheets on the sectional couch. "When the studio pays me."

My parents can't seem to absorb the fact that I have sold *Liza the Reluctant Lemming*. That it is actually going to be airing on cable television. That Excess is developing *Liza the Reluctant Lemming* as a series.

"But have you thought about getting a job, Liza, or moving back to New York, where you belong?" says my father, flipping through *Bride* magazine.

"They need me out here, for script conferences, meetings and things."

"For a cartoon?"

"Dad, do you realize that I am going to get a check for *Liza the Reluctant Lemming* that will be more than I made in an entire year working at that law firm?"

My father looks concerned. "Are you going to be responsible for paying the taxes on it?"

"Can't you just pretend to act a little impressed?"

"Liza, of course he's impressed," says my mother. "We both are."

"Liza," asks my father, "are you still doing astronomy?"

"Astrology, Dad, astrology. And no, I'm not." I turn to my mother. "Listen, Mom, I had this dream."

"I had a dream," booms out my father, impersonating Martin Luther King.

"Harold."

"Okay, okay, I'll be quiet."

"Well, it was about Gregor. We were in Pamplona and he was gored by a bull. And I ran after him and put Mole and Toad in the coffin."

"Mole and Toad?"

"You know, from *Wind in the Willows*. So Mom, what do you think it means?"

My mother shoves a pillow into a pillowcase. "Well off the top of my head, I'd say that there's a lot of anger there, and a feeling of revenge."

I fluff up the pillow. "But if I'm angry, why do I put Mole and Toad in the coffin?"

"Well, you know, everyone in the dream is you. So, maybe you're burying something from your childhood."

"Look at these dresses, they look like tablecloths." My father points to a lavishly embroidered wedding gown. "Who would wear that?"

AS I PREDICTED, my parents overcome all protests about having the wedding at their house.

"But I've always dreamed one of you girls would get married in the garden. It'll be a beautiful, sunny, fall day and you'll be so happy."

Bette pleads. "But Mom, Lawrence and I have already decided this."

My mother looks so pained, my sister crumbles almost immediately.

"Okay, okay, I'll convince Lawrence, somehow, and we'll have it in New York."

ALL OF A sudden, there is a huge hurry and the wedding is next weekend. "What's the rush?" I ask. "Everyone knows she's pregnant."

"Well, Lawrence's family is very conservative," says my mother. "We have to hurry up before Bette starts showing."

"It's too late for that. Anyway, how conservative can they be? They haven't disowned Tad, and he's gay. I don't think a little shotgun wedding is going to faze them."

"It's not a shotgun wedding, Liza," says my mother, acting shocked, as though she has suddenly been transformed into Emily Post.

My sister and I pore over cookbooks to plan the menu. My mother comes in.

"*Silver Palate:* poached salmon with dill sauce," says my sister. "Very elegant."

"Martha Stewart," I say, pointing at a glossy photo of waiters carrying around trays of canapés. "Stuffed pea pods with St. Andre cheese."

"I was thinking more of a buffet," says my mother.

My sister and I groan in unison.

"Mom, I just have one request," says my sister. "No hummus."

"But everyone loves hummus."

Bette holds firm. "It's nonnegotiable."

217

My mother and sister compromise on a local caterer although my mother doesn't think there's going to be enough food, so she wants to whip up a few things herself.

Lawrence's parents are taking care of the photographers, the flowers and the honeymoon.

Chapter twenty-one

DRIVING FROM THE airport up to my parents' house, I start to realize how much time has gone by. In LA, it's hard to believe time is passing, but here, the leaves are bright orange and red and you can't escape it. I never liked the changing of the leaves, never had a desire to go drive off to Vermont and watch the leaves in that Technicolor moment before they die. I've always preferred the bare winter trees. The fall colors are too bright and intrusive. When my parents start talking about how beautiful the leaves are, between sad folk songs and loud political commentaries on National Public Radio, I pretend to be asleep.

"LIZA COME HERE. Help me with the spinach pies."

It's the day before the big event, and I am in my mother's kitchen making extra hors d'oeuvres that we don't need.

"First, get me some dill from the garden."

219

I go outside to pick the dill. I walk around the house. My father must have been landscaping like crazy since the last time I was here, because there are several new pathways circling in front of the house. I walk along one pathway until I come to a little fountain with a fat stone Buddha in it taking a shower. I grab a penny from my pocket and throw it in. I wish . . .

"Liza!" I hear my mother calling.

"I'm coming." I go back into the kitchen.

My mother and I caress sheets of flaky phyllo dough with golden melted butter.

When I look at my mother I think of her in Sweden with Sven. My father working late. Me lying in my bath, reading a mystery novel, getting scared, the water growing cold around me.

"Liza what's the matter with you today? Is it Bette getting married?"

"No."

"Something's wrong."

"I was thinking about what you told me. About Sweden."

"I only told you because I thought it would help you and Gregor. You can't be upset at something that happened twenty years ago."

"Well, I am. I mean, what were you thinking? I take that back, I don't want to know."

"Your father and I worked that all out. Years ago."

"This isn't about him, it's about me. My feelings. Me. Liza."

My mother pauses, little drips of butter from the pastry brush falling on the white table.

I get the big blue sponge and wipe out the yellow butter dots.

"Oh Liza, you were always so sensitive."

"I don't even know if this is about Sven. It's just that everything seems so fragile. Look at this phyllo dough." I touch a piece I haven't buttered and it starts to break apart like a scroll of ancient papyrus. "If you look away for a moment, the whole thing crumbles. You find a pair of black underwear in a bed and your whole life changes."

"You found black underwear in your bed?"

"No, it's just an example."

"Liza, this is totally fixable." My mother grabs the pastry brush and quickly covers the crumbling phyllo dough with streams of butter. "Look, it's fine now. We'll put the spinach in and no one will be able to tell the difference."

I WAKE UP early on the day of the wedding. Looking out the window I see, as my mother predicted, a crisp sunny day. I put on my dress. Yesterday, my mother and I went into town and bought it. It's not my usual type of dress. For one thing it's not black. It's a violet color, very simple. My mother wanted to buy it for me, but I charged it on my Visa card with the biggest limit.

Tad comes over early to help. "I had to escape my parents. They're driving me crazy."

"That's their job."

We put up decorations and unfold chairs for the ceremony.

My sister has found a girl she went to high school with to perform the ceremony. She's Unitarian, so no one, or everyone, will get offended.

My sister is getting ready in my mother's bathroom. I help her with her makeup.

"There, just a little eye shadow and some blush."

"Don't put on too much."

"Don't worry."

I help her put on the dress. It's made of antique lace with tiny pearl buttons. We picked it up in LA at a costume shop.

221

"It's beautiful."

"Do I look pregnant?" asks my sister, smoothing her mostly flat stomach.

"No, just like you need to do a few sit-ups."

"Really?"

"You look perfect."

MY SISTER HAS a bouquet of wildflowers, not from the garden. These are specially treated flowers that stay fresh and just look wild.

I sit next to my parents at the wedding. My brother is in Indonesia now so he couldn't make the wedding. But he FedExed Bette a special blue stone with magical properties.

MY MOTHER AND father hold hands during the ceremony. Lawrence reads a poem by Yeats that starts "When you are old and gray and full of sleep. . . ." It's from a book of poetry I gave Gregor for his birthday. I keep thinking about Gregor. I've been so angry with him, I haven't realized how much I miss him. But now, watching my sister and Lawrence, I think about how we'll never do this, say that we'll be together forever and ever. I think about how I would help him with his acting exercises, how we used to lie in bed at night and hug, how jealous I was before there was any reason to be. I always said I never wanted to get married, ever since I can remember, and now I can see that it's a lie. I just knew that I didn't have that kind of faith. I try to imagine what kind of wedding Gregor and I would have. I always used to say that if I did ever get married, the only way I could bring myself to do it would be flying to Las Vegas on impulse and getting married by an Elvis impersonator. As my sister and Lawrence say their vows, I imagine it's me and Gregor, standing in front of an Elvis impersonator, with "Don't Be Cruel" playing in the background.

When the minister pronounces them husband and wife,

my mother cries. I pat her on the arm and give her my package of Kleenex. Then I start to cry and have to take some back. My father shakes his head at our foolishness, but he looks kind of emotional too.

AT THE RECEPTION, it is amazing how well my parents and Lawrence's get along. My father and Lawrence's father share a mutual interest in landscaping and our mothers share a love of folk dance.

"Why didn't you introduce us earlier?" my mother asks Bette as she swings around Lawrence's mother in the intricate steps of an Israeli folk dance.

Lawrence's mother is in a pale pink Chanel suit and my mother is in a dark purple gauzy garment that swirls around her as she dances. Tad and I stand off to the side, shaking our heads in amazement.

We watch Miranda, wearing a red suit with a huge peplum, trying to impress various people who have no idea who she is.

"Isn't it considered bad taste to wear blood red to a wedding?" I ask Tad.

"Deplorable. Oh by the way, Liza, I meant to tell you earlier, but I've got some contracts for you to sign later. I got you a good deal with those people at Excess, especially in terms of foreign rights."

"Well, I definitely believe that foreigners should have rights. Tad, speak English. How much money did I get?"

"Well, I have a check for the advance. This is just for the first five episodes. And if they actually air *Liza the Reluctant Lemming*, then we get a percentage."

"What do you mean if they actually air it? It's not definite?"

"At this point, it's just an option to air it. It's cable after all. But if they don't you are still entitled to a kill fee."

"How appropriate."

223

"Liza don't worry."

"You might as well tell me not to breathe."

"Do you want me to give it to you now, or somewhere more private?"

"This is fine."

Tad hands me the check. I look at it. For a moment, I can't really make out the numbers. They are only digits with no relation to each other. I didn't exactly know what to expect, but I am holding a check for sixty-five thousand dollars. My hands start to shake.

"I can't believe this."

"Liza, I'm sorry, but I had to deduct my commission and there were a few expenses, FedEx, telephone, you know."

"You don't get it. I'm not upset, I'm in shock. Thank you." I give Tad a big hug.

"Stop, you're wrinkling my linen."

We clink our glasses of champagne. "Here's to my lawyer and my brother-in-law in-law."

Tad pretends to choke. "Don't remind me."

"You love it."

"Hey Liza, isn't that Gregor? Over by the bar?"

I squint in the sun and make out a blur by the bar. Yes it's him. It's Gregor, and he looks just like he did in my dream.

"Tad, do you believe in the significance of dreams?"

"Depends on the dream."

I TRY TO go to Gregor, but people keep stopping me on the way, grabbing my arm, smiling at me.

"Doesn't your sister look beautiful?" says a former student of my mother's, grabbing my arm.

"She's radiant," I agree.

"Who made these spinach pies?" demands an old, very wrinkled lady.

"Delicious."

"What a beautiful day for a wedding."

I wade past them and see my sister, who is hurrying toward the house.

I run over to her. "Bette, you're leaving?"

"Our flight to Barcelona is in two hours."

"Bette, listen. Gregor's here!!"

"I know, I invited him."

"You what??"

"Look, I thought it would be a . . . Don't be mad."

"I'm not mad. It's just too weird. With all these people."

"Why don't you go talk to him in the cottage?"

"But that's for you and Lawrence. It's the honeymoon suite."

"But we're leaving, so . . ."

"Barcelona. Isn't that where those Gaudi buildings are?" I hear Lawrence calling her in the background. "This is it, Bette. You better go." I kiss her, smearing her carefully made-up cheek with my dark lipstick. " I try to rub it off with my finger.

"It's okay. It doesn't matter."

"I can't believe you're married. You're not going to change, are you?"

"Of course not."

"Call me the minute you get back from Barcelona."

My sister looks over at Gregor. "But where are you going to be?"

"LA. I'm going to stay at a hotel and order lots of room service. I'm rich now. Look at this." I pull the check out of my bag and try to point at the amount but someone pulls her away.

I FIND GREGOR IN front of the herb garden.

I tell him, "I had a horrible dream about you. You were in Pamplona, with the bulls."

"I've always wanted to go to Pamplona."

225

"You got gored, but there wasn't a lot of blood."

"That sounds unpleasant."

"I'm glad you're alive."

Gregor puts his hand up and tries to smooth my hair behind my ears.

"You're smoothing me."

"I missed you Liza."

I feel a burst of warmth melting the icicle inside my heart. "I missed you too."

I see my parents and Lawrence's parents heading toward us in a clump.

I grab Gregor's hand. "Hurry, come with me."

We run to the cottage as if we are being chased by wolves. We sneak behind the house where the wedding guests can't see us, run along the side of the yard where we're camouflaged by the huge rock walls my father has been building. We arrive at the little cottage, panting.

Tad and I had decorated the cottage earlier for my sister and Lawrence before we realized they were leaving right away. We spent all morning cleaning and Tad even killed a centipede, but now it is as if I have never seen it before. There is a trail of red rosebuds leading to the bed, and the bed is heaped with all the pillows Tad and I could salvage from my mother's brief needlepoint phase, pillows embroidered with flowers and unicorns, velvety throw pillows in dark purple and reds.

Gregor and I take off our clothes quickly, silently, urgently. We kiss and kiss and kiss, running our hands all over each other until they meet and intertwine. Each part of his body is like a new continent. I forget all about the people outside at the wedding. I forget about everything that has happened. For this one moment, I don't worry about what's going to happen. It is just the two of us. We roll and roll around the soft bed until we have to get even closer, until I hear myself moaning and Gregor making that roaring bear sound he made the first time we ever made love.

Once we cool down, I retrieve the pâté and cheese that Tad put in the miniature fridge for Bette and Lawrence.

"You know this doesn't mean I'm moving back to New York right away."

Gregor strokes my hair. "Okay."

"Or that I forgive you. Because I could never forgive you."

"I don't expect you to."

"It's just that seeing you in that coffin made me realize that I want to spend whatever little time I have left with you."

"Liza, you're only thirty-two!"

"I'm almost thirty-three. Listen, just because you're the actor doesn't mean I'm not allowed to be melodramatic once in a while." I smile.

There is a knocking on the door.

"Do you think they know we're in here?" asks Gregor, rolling off the bed and picking up his pants.

"I doubt it. Maybe someone wants to see the cottage."

The knocking gets louder.

"Liza, I know you're in there."

"Oh, it's Tad."

I throw my dress over my head and let him in the door.

"Tad, my hero!"

Tad looks around disapprovingly at the disarray. "Quite the little love nest you've got here."

"You want some pâté?"

"No, you have to come with me right now, this instant. Sorry, Gregor."

I start picking rose petals out of my hair. "What's so urgent?"

"Bette's throwing her bouquet!!"

We emerge into the late-afternoon sunlight. Everyone is

227

crowded around the steps of the porch, single women in the front. Bette has changed into a short dress.

She turns around to throw her wildflower bouquet.

"I can't believe she's doing this," says Tad. "I love it. It's so retro."

"You're just jealous."

I move quickly toward the front of the crowd and put my hands out to catch it.

Reading Group Guide

THE PERFECT ELIZABETH

LIBBY SCHMAIS

1. In the first few chapters, Liza buys Bette a book on meeting men, drags her to a matchmaker, and takes her to a singles party. Why is it so important to Liza that Bette be in a relationship?

2. Bette has devoted her entire academic career to researching food in the English novel. What is behind this obsession? What role does food play in the novel as a whole?

3. Why does Liza continue walking dogs for Amelia and Gwendolyn?

4. What is the significance of the children's story that Liza writes within the novel? How does *Liza the Lemming* resemble Liza's life?

5. Why does Liza feel that she and Bette are two parts of one perfect Elizabeth? Does that perception change throughout the novel?

6. What roles do Liza and Bette play in their family? What happens when their roles change?

7. Liza says near the beginning of the story, "Everything I know how to do well is useless. Everything I don't know is impossible." Why does Liza believe this?

8. Are the parents a negative or positive influence on the sisters? How have they shaped the sisters?

9. What happens to Liza during her stay in Los Angeles? How does her perspective change?

10. The book ends ~~on an uplifting note, but do~~ you believe that Liza and Bette live ~~...~~ or and Lawrence? Where do you ~~...~~ ears' time?

For more readi~~ng...~~ r.stmartins.com